SHADOW WARRIOR
A Jake Adams International Espionage Thriller #15

by
Trevor Scott

United States of America

Also by Trevor Scott

<u>Karl Adams Espionage Thriller Series</u>
The Man from Murmansk (#1)
Siberian Protocol (#2)

<u>Max Kane Series</u>
Truth or Justice (#1)
Stolen Honor (#2)
Relative Impact (#3)

<u>Jake Adams International Espionage Thriller Series</u>
Fatal Network (#1)
Extreme Faction (#2)
The Dolomite Solution (#3)
Vital Force (#4)
Rise of the Order (#5)
The Cold Edge (#6)
Without Options (#7)
The Stone of Archimedes (#8)
Lethal Force (#9)
Rising Tiger (#10)
Counter Caliphate (#11)
Gates of Dawn (#12)
Counter Terror (#13)

Covert Network (#14)
Shadow Warrior (#15)
Sedition (#16)

<u>The Tony Caruso Mystery Series</u>
Boom Town (#1)
Burst of Sound (#2)
Running Game (#3)

<u>The Chad Hunter Espionage Thriller Series</u>
Hypershot (#1)
Global Shot (#2)
Cyber Shot (#3)

<u>The Keenan Fitzpatrick Mystery Series</u>
Isolated (#1)
Burning Down the House (#2)
Witness to Murder (#3)

<u>Other Mysteries and Thrillers</u>
Cantina Valley
Edge of Delirium
Strong Conviction
Fractured State (A Novella)
The Nature of Man

Discernment
Way of the Sword
Drifting Back
The Dawn of Midnight
The Hobgoblin of the Redwoods
Duluthians: A Collection of Short Stories

This is a work of fiction. All characters and events portrayed in this novel are fictitious and not intended to represent real people or places. All rights reserved. No part of this book may be reproduced in any manner whatsoever without written permission of the author.

SHADOW WARRIOR
Copyright © 2017 by Trevor Scott
United States of America
trevorscott.com

Cover image of shooter by abishome
Background cover image by author

1

Innsbruck, Austria

April showers had given way to a Mayday downpour, enveloping the downtown region of this Tirolian city in a deep funk as late evening moved toward midnight. Hunkered under an overhang two blocks from The Golden Roof, the woman in dark clothes shoved her hands into the pockets of her bulky light jacket. She had cut out her right pocket, so her hand rested on the butt of her Glock 19 on her right hip.

Anica Senka had been working undercover for the past week, so she carried no Austrian Polizei identification. In fact, she had no purse—only a driver's license with a fake name. Officially she still worked for the Polizei, but she had recently taken a liaison job with a newly formed task force of EUROPOL, the European Police Office, the law enforcement agency of the European Union. After a short briefing at EUROPOL headquarters in The Hague, Netherlands, Anica had come back to Austria to infiltrate the Serbian crime organization.

Whispering quietly, Anica said in German, "We couldn't have met in a coffee shop?"

The comm earbud in her right ear buzzed slightly. Then her contact's voice said, "We were lucky to get any meeting at all."

She knew this, of course. Because of her Serbian language skills, she had been selected to infiltrate a potential criminal organization that was purportedly headed by a former Serbian military officer. Although this man had worked directly under Slobodan Milosevic, the former Serbian President who had been tried and convicted for war crimes, for some reason many of his brutal military officers had been cleared of wrongdoing. Nevertheless, many of these disgraced officers could no longer step foot in Serbia for fear of death by the remaining families who had been brutalized during the

90s. So, they had emigrated to other parts of Europe—like Austria.

Anica knew all too well the horrors of the Balkan Wars of the 90s. Both of her parents had been killed, and she had been forced to flee to Austria as a young girl, living with a distant relative. But that escape had brought her into an equally brutal home life, where this relative had tried to abuse her mentally and sexually. She had been lucky, though, helped by a kind neighbor, who had eventually placed her in the home of a local Polizei family. Anica had repaid her gratitude by becoming a Polizei officer to help others who needed help.

"He's not coming," Anica said softly, and then wiped moisture from her face. The overhang only brought her a little relief from the relentless rain, which seemed to come down in sideways sheets.

"Look again," her contact said. "Far end of the lane by The Golden Roof."

The Goldenes Dachl, or Golden Roof, was the city's main tourist attraction, and sat just a couple of blocks south of the Inn River. During nice days, the square in front of this attraction would be filled with tourists. But with the hour and the inclement weather, only a couple of people hurried from bar to bar. Anica had dubbed these European locations terrorist attractions. Locations that were nearly impossible to defend properly in a free society.

Anica finally saw the man lingering down the square, so she moved out into the main deluge and shuffled toward her target. Over the past week this man, Bogdan Maravich, had come close to giving her the name of the next man up the rung. He had been a young Serbian private during the war, but was now unemployed officially, collecting government assistance, while he was paid under the table by the Serbian Mafia. At least that's what Anica suspected. This Bogdan fellow had a face only an ermine mother could love, Anica thought. His mottled, leathery complexion was a roadmap of self-abuse through drink and smoke.

Moving in closer, Anica felt anxious. Something wasn't right. She could tell. She had always had this innate ability to feel danger near. Part of that, she knew, was her survival instinct from the war. Yet, these feelings of hers had come in handy as a Polizei officer, keeping her safe for the past ten years.

"Moving in," she said softly.

All she got back was static. A lot of static. Something was wrong with her earbud. Perhaps the water had shorted something.

She met the man and the two of them didn't embrace or shake hands. They kept their distance as they wandered together toward the river down *Herzog-Friedrich Strasse*. Neither of them said a word until they reached the bridge over the Inn River. Lights from the colorful buildings across the river shimmered on the rain-swollen water that cut through the city like a scoliotic spine. For a second, Anica let the beauty of the yellow, green, blue and orange multi-story buildings distract her from the man next to her as they walked toward the pedestrian walk to the side of the road on the bridge. A chill came over her as rain pelted the exposed skin on her neck.

"This is dangerous business," the man said in Serbian.

"I am just looking for a job," she said.

"The boss does not hire just anyone," he said, and then lit a cigarette. He offered one to Anica, but she waved him off.

"My father worked for Milosevic," she said in her defense. Not a total lie. In truth, both of her parents had worked for that man in various capacities in his government. Which is probably what had gotten them killed.

Her contact laughed as he drew in smoke to his lungs. Then he let out a stream of smoke and said, "You either worked for that man or you worked against him. Either way, you would now be dead, in jail, or in exile."

"Like your boss?" she asked. She needed names, and this man had been reluctant to give her anything in the past week. She suspected he wanted sex from her, but she wasn't willing to go that far for any case.

Now they crossed the street and entered the walkway along the road on the main bridge crossing the Inn River. A few cars still sat parked along the side of the road on the bridge. For a Monday evening in this desperate rain, not my locals were out and about.

"Where are we going?" Anica said in German, hoping her people were still monitoring her comm. "What are we doing on the bridge?"

"Zoran Petrovic wants to meet you," he said, sticking to Serbian.

She repeated the name in case her contact had not picked up the conversation. "I thought he was dead."

The Serb stopped and grasped her left arm. She considered pulling her gun, but the man's grasp did not seem overly aggressive.

"Oh, he is alive," he said. "I think he cannot be killed."

Finally, she heard garbled voices through her earbud. She wanted to ask him to repeat the last transmission, but knew that would be stupid.

When she noticed the car slowly coming toward them from the other side of the river, she wasn't sure if those inside were with the Austrian Polizei or this man's organization. Her right hand instinctively grasped her gun.

"What is the matter?" the Serb asked.

Before she could answer, the dark Audi picked up speed and swerved across both lanes toward them.

Anica drew her weapon and shoved the Serb away from her. Instead of jumping the curb, the car turned sharply and skid to a halt. Flashes broke the darkness, followed by at least a dozen loud reports from two guns.

Reflexively, she dove to the ground while she fired at the car. The Serb also hit the pavement, but he did so reluctantly, taking several bullets to his body. Crawling quickly, Anica found momentary safety behind the back of a car. They had her dead if they wanted, she thought. She had no place to go.

Then it came to her. She emptied her magazine as she ran to the railing, the slide locking back on her Glock just as she hoisted herself over the metal rail.

As she seemed to float through the darkness, Anica twisted her legs together and crossed her arms over her chest just as she hit the water.

The impact of the icy water took her breath away momentarily as her body sunk under the surface. Then her feet hit the bottom and she shoved with all her might to rise back to the surface. She wasn't sure if she could hold her breath much longer, when she finally surfaced and took in a mixture of air and water.

Her body went numb as she was drawn swiftly downstream through the darkness.

2

Pico Island, The Azores
Six days later

The waves were nearly non-existent this Sunday morning as Jake Adams sat on a rock looking to the south at the Atlantic. His fishing rod sat in a fissure in the rocks, his line taught as the outgoing tide pulled his bait further out to sea.

Fishing was still fresh for Jake since his self-imposed exile on this remote island chain a few months back. He had left a lot behind with the death of

Alexandra in Calabria, and his subsequent placement of his daughter Emma in Montana with his siblings. Emma was better off with his brother and sister. She would be safe, he knew.

Jake had first tried to drink himself to death in Iceland for a while. Iceland was beautiful, but it was also too damn cold. So, after his last major mission in South America, Sirena had suggested a little warmer climate to the south of Iceland, and Jake had agreed.

He looked at his reflection in the water and almost didn't recognize himself. His hair was longer than normal, and much more silver than black these days. He shaved about once a week now, and was three days in from his last trim. Even his facial stubble seemed more gray than black. He wasn't sure if he liked this new look, even though Sirena seemed to think he looked more distinguished. Whatever the hell that meant.

When he could no longer ignore what was coming, he pulled his 9mm Glock from inside his jacket and swiveled quickly around, pointing his gun at a surprised woman, who raised her hands immediately. She was perhaps in her early forties or late thirties. It was hard for Jake to tell with blondes.

"Herr Adams?" the woman said. "Jake Adams?" She had a strong German accent.

Jake got up and moved closer to the woman. She had been a real looker in her younger years, but time had added a few pounds to her midsection and wrinkles of consternation seemed to be deeply ingrained across her forehead, as if she were in a constant state of wonder.

"Sabine Bauer," Jake said. "What brings you to my island?"

The woman tried on a smile, failing from lack of practice. "I believe the Portuguese still own The Azores."

Jake waved his left hand in the general area in front of him. "Except for this small piece of the coast."

When Sirena appeared from behind some small bushes, her own Glock pointed at the woman, Jake said, "It's all right, Sirena. This is Sabine Bauer, the newest Kriminal Hauptkommisar of the Austrian state of Tirol."

"You know this?" Sabine asked.

"I know that the Austrian Polizei has been trying to get in touch with me for the past few days," Jake said. "I finally allowed you to find me. But I'm still not sure why."

Sabine tried to smile again. "We met years ago."

"I know," Jake said. "You were sleeping with Hermann Jung to rise up the chain."

"That was a mistake," Sabine said.

"Which part? Sleeping with Jung or taking his job?"

"He took retirement," she said. "He's divorced and living in Kitzbuhel."

"Good place for him," Jake said.

"He had two heart attacks."

"I didn't realize he had a heart."

"We didn't end things well," Sabine said.

"You came to your senses and he moved to Kitzbuhel," Jake said. "Sounds like things are as they should be. Now, what brings you all the way from Innsbruck to my remote island?"

"If I had your phone number, I could have simply called you," she said. "But I'm not sure you would have listened."

Jake returned his gun to its holster inside his jacket. "You look like you could use a cup of coffee."

"I could," Sabine said. "It's not easy getting here."

Smiling, Jake said, "That's kind of the point, Sabine."

The three of them wandered up the path to the small single-story house. Just then, Jake remembered he still had his line in the water. He shrugged it off.

Sirena found some glasses and started to make them each a cappuccino. Jake sat in a leather chair with a pleasant view of the road leading up to the place and the ocean. Even though the Austrian Polizei officer had parked down the hill a hundred meters, Sirena would have been able to see the woman coming from miles away. That was Jake's reason for renting the fully-furnished place.

Sabine sat across from Jake, her hands nervously on her knees.

In a moment, the first cappuccino was done and Sirena handed it to the Austrian cop.

"Thank you," Sabine said, and then sipped the coffee. "This is very good. Columbian?"

"Costa Rican," Jake said. "I know a guy."

Neither said a word until Jake accepted his cappuccino from Sirena, who then took up a position across the room, standing and listening. Jake could tell Sirena was suspicious of this other woman. She knew some of Jake's background, but not all of it. Perhaps she assumed he had slept with this Austrian cop.

Finally, Jake said, "Okay, now you can tell me why the Austrian Polizei has been looking for me."

Sabine hesitated, her eyes shifting toward Sirena and then settling on Jake. "You have a very good reputation with our organization. Not to mention with the Austrian government and the royal family."

Jake wasn't sure if this praise was her attempt at blowing smoke, but he sipped his cappuccino and let her fling praise.

Sabine continued, "Anyway, the Polizei would like to hire you as a consultant."

He shifted his gaze for a second at Sirena, who seemed bored if not completely indifferent. "For what purpose?"

"Are you familiar with Europol?"

"Sounds like a porn star," Jake quipped.

"Hardly. They are the European Police Office, a law enforcement agency of the European Union, with headquarters in The Hague, Netherlands."

He knew about them. They were like the junior park rangers of law enforcement. That was all the EU needed was its own cops, he thought. "What about them?"

"Since their inception less than ten years ago, they have not been involved with cross border investigations," Sabine said. "They have simply been a coordinating agency. They only have about a thousand employees, and those are mostly analysts at their headquarters. Anyway, they have started to push their traditional agenda, becoming more like Interpol."

Jake was still confused. "How does this impact me?"

After finishing her cappuccino and placing her cup on the coffee table, Sabine said, "We were asked to designate two of our Polizei officers with Europol as resources they could use on cross-border investigations. These two officers were working a case dealing with an international criminal organization in Innsbruck."

"Seriously? Innsbruck?" Jake asked.

"Not headquartered there," Sabine corrected. "But with a franchise there."

Jake shrugged. "Would you get to the point?"

Sabine nodded. "Of course. One of the officers was Anica Senka."

Now Jake knew why he might be interested. "I've known Anica since she was a young girl."

"That's what I was made to believe," Sabine said, before a long pause. Finally, she said, "Anica is missing."

Jake sat forward in his chair. "Missing? How?"

"Because of her Serbian background, she was working undercover to infiltrate this group."

Serbs? Damn! Jake had dealt with these folks in the past, and it had nearly gotten him killed. "Continue."

"She got in a shoot-out with someone on the Innbrucke Bridge," Sabine said. "The Serb she was meeting was killed, but we think Anica ended up in the river."

"Were you monitoring her communications?" Jake asked.

"Of course. But there was a problem with her comm. It was raining very hard that night. It probably shorted out."

Not likely, Jake thought. Most of those units worked underwater. "What do you want me to do?"

"Find Anica," Sabine said.

"What makes you think I can find her if the entire Austrian Polizei can't do so?"

"Good question. My boss in Vienna has told us to suspend our search."

"Why?"

"Because it was a Europol operation."

"But she works for Austrian Polizei," Jake reminded her.

"Technically she was on loan to them."

Something wasn't working for Jake. "This is bullshit. It sounds like the Polizei is abandoning one of its own."

A grimace spread across Sabine's face. "My hands are tied. I am doing the best I can."

Okay, now Jake had an idea. She had been forced to stand down. "Does your boss know you're here?"

She shook her head. "Not exactly. As you know, Tirol doesn't always agree with Vienna."

That was an understatement. "So, I will be alone on this endeavor," Jake said.

"I can't officially sanction you to do anything," Sabine agreed.

Jake didn't need anything from them. "As long as your people stay out of my way, that's all I can ask. But I'll need to speak with the other officer she was working with that night."

"He doesn't know much," Sabine said. Then she pulled out a jump drive from inside her jacket and placed it on the coffee table. "Everything we know is on that."

Jake slid the jump drive closer to him. "Have you been to her apartment?"

"Of course." She got up to leave. "Her apartment has a keypad entry. The code is on the jump drive as well."

"Other than my relationship with Anica, why me?" Jake asked.

"You helped her in the past," Sabine said. "I'm hoping you will help her again."

Sabine headed toward the door and Jake followed her to let her out.

"I'll do what I can," Jake said.

The Austrian nodded her head and left.

Jake turned to Sirena, who had kept quiet for the entire visit. "What do you think?" he asked.

"She's not telling you everything," Sirena said.

He laughed. "That was obvious. What else?"

"How do you know this young Anica?"

"It's a long story. But essentially, when her parents died in the Balkan War, Anica was sent to Innsbruck to live with a distant relative. This man abused her mentally and physically. When he tried to make sexual advances, she came to me. She lived in the building next to mine along the Inn River. I had a little discussion with her relative."

"I'll bet," Sirena said with a smirk.

"Then I got her placed with one of my friends in the Austrian Polizei," he said.

"It sounds like you might have saved her life."

"I don't know about that. I saw a young child in need and I did what I could to help her. We've kept in touch over the years, but not much in the past two years."

"Well, you've been kind of busy moving from Italy to Iceland to The Azores."

That was no excuse, he knew. But too often life got in the way of old relationships.

"Are you coming with me?" he asked her.

Sirena put her hands on her hips and said, "This place is beautiful, Jake, but quaint gets old after a few months. I'm in."

"All right. Get packed and ready to move out. See if you can get Carlos Gomez to lend us his jet." Jake headed toward the door.

"Where are you going?"

"I left a line in the water." He left and ran down to the ocean to retrieve his rod and reel, hoping a large fish had not pulled it into the sea.

3

Innsbruck, Austria

Thanks to the use of the jet owned by Spanish billionaire Carlos Gomez, Jake and Sirena were able to travel from The Azores to Austria without having to go through normal airport security, which allowed them to bring their handguns.

As Monday evening approached, Jake and Sirena walked from their downtown hotel along the river to the Innbrucke Bridge near The Golden Roof. Once on the bridge, Jake stopped about midway across and turned back toward the old town of the city. Lights lit the buildings with a bright sepia, but he remembered Sabine Bauer say that it had been raining hard the night Anica was forced into the river.

"What are you thinking?" Sirena asked.

"I'm thinking that Anica should have never agreed to a meeting here," he said.

"She didn't. The Polizei report said the meeting was in the Golden Roof square."

"I know. But that had obviously changed. For some reason, they walked out here."

She leaned against the thick metal railing and considered the river. "The water is really high. Could she have simply drowned?"

That was a possibility, he knew. But he had to believe she was still alive. "I don't think so. She carries two phones—one for work and her private smart phone. The work phone shut down the night Anica went missing."

"When?"

"About an hour after going into the river, which is why the Polizei could not track her," Jake said.

"They must know about her private line."

"They do. But the Austrian government has rules. And those rules don't allow for tracking of personal phones without a court order."

"And they can't get that under these circumstances?"

Jake turned to Sirena and smiled. "Why do you think Sabine came to me? She knows I don't have to comply with Austrian law."

"Not to mention that your benefactor, Carlos Gomez, happens to run one of the largest cell phone communications companies in Europe."

"That helps."

She touched the leather on his sleeve. "You've been holding out on me."

"I need you to think big picture," he said. "Where would a young woman go after almost getting killed?"

"First, you tell me why you think she didn't drown in the river."

Jake shrugged. "Her private phone has come back on line a couple of times in the past week."

Sirena looked confused. "Why would she make that mistake?"

"It's no mistake. I think she's leaving us bread crumbs."

"She can't possibly know you're looking for her."

"No. But she might believe someone else is. Someone she trusts. Let's go to her apartment."

Anica Senka lived just six blocks away on the left bank of the Inn River, a few blocks in from the water. Her apartment was in a three-story walk-up. The first story was occupied by a small bar, which looked almost empty from the street. Anica lived on the third floor with a view of the mountains to the south of the city.

Jake expected to find crime-scene tape across her door, but there was none of that. Although the building was old, the doors and locks had been upgraded.

He punched in the four-digit code to the lock and lowered the lever. Just as Jake was about to shove the door inward, he heard a noise, which caused him to draw his Glock. Sirena did the same.

Shoving the door inward, Jake hit the light and swept his gun until he locked on a target—a young man with a flashlight.

"Put your hands on the back of your head," Jake said in German.

The young man in his early thirties did as Jake instructed. Then he said in English, "You are Jake Adams."

"No, I'm Schinderhannes. Who are you?"

"Polizei Officer Johann Gruber. My identification is in my inside jacket pocket."

Jake kept his gun on the man while Sirena came around him and reached inside the man's jacket until she found his badge and a Glock on his right hip. Officer Gruber looked like a poster child for the Arian ideal. His blond hair was cropped short on the sides, but the strip of hair on the top was a bit longer, held tight with enough product to hold up in a stiff breeze.

She checked the man's credentials and nodded to Jake.

"Where did you learn your English?" Jake asked. "It's almost perfect."

"Almost?" Johann asked.

"Well, you have some Texas inflections."

Johann smiled. "I was an exchange officer for a year in Dallas. Plus, I watch a lot of old American westerns."

Sirena handed the man his ID and gun.

But Jake still had his gun trained on the man. "Why are you here in Anica's apartment?"

"We were partners," Johann said.

Jake already knew this, since he had read Anica's service file. "Partners don't normally have access to apartments. Unless you were more than just partners."

Glancing about the apartment, Jake could see that someone had destroyed the place looking for something. Maybe looking for anything. The only thing they didn't do was rip the stuffing out of her furniture.

"Could you please put the gun away, Mister Adams. You're making me nervous."

"How do you know who I am?"

"Two reasons. Anica told me about you. How you had saved her as a child. And second, my boss, Sabine Bauer, said you would be coming here."

"So, why wait in the darkness?"

"I'm sorry about that. I was resting on her sofa when I heard footsteps in the hallway."

"And you assumed it was me and not the bad guys?" Jake asked. "That could have gotten you killed."

"I made a choice," Johann said. "If it was you and I had drawn my service weapon, you might have shot me, thinking I was a bad guy. If you happened to be a bad guy, I would have had to draw my weapon and hope to beat the man to the draw."

"You have been watching too many westerns," Jake reasoned.

Sirena chimed in, "He has a point."

Jake put his gun back in the holster under his left arm inside his leather jacket. "What do you know about Anica's disappearance?"

"I was with her that night. Monitoring her comm from my car a few blocks away."

"Then you led her into a trap," Jake said callously.

"No, sir," Johann said. "Her comm failed. I tried to tell her not to leave our target area in the square, but she obviously didn't hear me."

"Did you move in?"

Johann let out a heavy breath of air, shaking his head. "I did. But the shooting started before I got there."

"You saw the car?" Jake asked.

"Yes. I didn't get a license number. But I called it in to our headquarters."

"You didn't follow the car?"

"No. I had a choice to make. Follow the car or help Anica. I chose to help my partner."

Okay, maybe this young Polizei officer wasn't a total tool. He had made the same choice Jake would have made under those circumstances. "All right. So, you get to the scene and find a dead man. Anica's contact."

"Yes, sir." Johann closed his eyes slightly, as if remembering the events of that evening. Then he said, "At the time, I wasn't even sure that Anica had gone into the river. In retrospect, I thought she could have been kidnapped by those in the car. I questioned my decision to not follow the car."

"What changed your mind?" Jake asked.

"We found blood on the railing," Johann explained.

"Anica was injured?"

"No. It was her contact's blood. She must have touched him after he was shot. We also found blood on the back end of a car she hid behind as she shot at the killers."

This all made some sense. It wasn't the way Jake would have liked it to go down, especially the outcome of his young friend having to jump into the river to escape. But then a thought came to him. "Why didn't you have more backup?"

Johann now seemed a bit rattled. "This was a Europol operation. Our local Polizei office had nothing to do with it."

Jake now saw something in this young Polizei officer that he had not seen to this point. Johann Gruber had not just been Anica's partner, he had true feelings for Jake's young friend. And his involvement in her disappearance was eating him up inside. Jake had been there before himself.

"All right," Jake said. "What have you found of interest here? Did you destroy her place?"

Johann smiled. "It's what I didn't find. A few items are missing."

"Like what?"

"Her passport, her Europol identification, and a small bag with clothes."

"What about her Polizei ID?" Sirena asked.

"That was here," Johann said. "Our people took it on their first visit."

"Why take her Europol ID?" Sirena asked.

Jake took this. "Because she thought she might need it beyond Austria. Tell me more about your investigation into the Serbs."

Johann didn't get a chance to explain the investigation, as Jake got a text on his phone. He almost ignored it, but decided to see what it was. Not many had his number. Not even Anica had his private number. At least not until arriving in Innsbruck, when Jake sent her a couple of texts to her private phone.

Looking at his screen it simply said, 'Get out, Uncle Jake!' This came from an unknown number, but it could have been only one person. Only Anica Senka called him Uncle Jake.

"We have to go," Jake said sternly.

The three of them left and locked up Anica's apartment before heading downstairs. Jake kept his eyes open for anything unusual. Somehow, Anica knew they were in her apartment. She had to be close.

They got to the sidewalk in front of the bar and Jake grasped the young Polizei officer's arm. "Are you still on this Serbian connection?"

Johann said, "Of course."

"Do you have a car?"

Nodding, Johann said, "An Audi a block away."

"We could use a ride to our hotel."

"Certainly."

As they walked toward the Audi parked under trees up the block, Jake was the first to notice the car driving too slowly up the street. He zipped down his leather jacket and placed his hand on his Glock.

Glancing at Sirena, she also noticed the car and had her hand inside her purse ready to draw her weapon.

"Get ready, Johann," Jake said.

Stopping, Johann said, "For what."

Not having time to explain, Jake swept the legs out from the Austrian and drew his gun simultaneously once he noticed the windows come down on the car and the barrels appear. Then Jake went into a crouched shooting position.

Sirena was the first to shoot, peppering the car with a salvo of shots. Then Jake starting firing just as the flashes came from the car windows.

Next came chaos, as both sides continued to fire their guns. Seconds later, the car sped away and turned right at the first corner.

Jake checked on Johann, who was in shock on the sidewalk. He had not even drawn his weapon.

"Everyone alright?" Jake asked, reaching his hand down to Johann.

"What the hell just happened?" Johann asked, getting a hand from Jake and wiping off his jeans.

Sirena put her gun back in her purse.

"This is normally a quiet Tirol city," Johann said. "Now we have two drive-by shootings in a week. That's crazy."

Jake reflected on some of the incidents he had experienced in this city, and he knew that Johann was partially correct. Violence like this was rare, but seemed to be on the increase across Europe.

"We had an old saying in the Air Force," Jake said. "You caught the most flak when you were directly over the target."

"What is flak?" Johann asked.

"In this case, it's bullets. We're on to something. Let's go. I know a few Serbs in this town who might know what we're looking for."

"What are we looking for?" Johann wanted to know.

"Exactly."

"But we must wait for the Polizei to arrive," Johann pled.

Sirens could be heard in the distance now.

"No. You drive and I'll text Sabine and explain what happened."

They piled into the Austrian's Audi and he pulled out.

4

There was no Little Serbia or Balkan section of Innsbruck, but there was a district on the east side of town near the main train station where many of the more recent immigrants seemed to congregate. Although the city was normally sedate, Jake knew about the recent trouble with immigrants perpetrating rape like it was a perfectly acceptable practice. The Austrian people, along with the government, had reached a tipping point. Finally, they had started to take a hard look at allowing people into Austria.

Jake had lived along the Inn River in Innsbruck for many years after leaving the CIA, so he knew the city quite well. He had also dealt with the Serbs in the past, especially while dealing with the Anica Senka incident years ago.

One of the more influential Serbs in town ran a Balkan restaurant two blocks from the Innsbruck *Hauptbahnhof.* A passenger train pulled slowly out of the main train station now as Jake walked down the street toward the restaurant. He had left Sirena and Johann in the car with instructions to call Sabine Bauer to explain what had happened with the shooting.

Jake turned up the block and could see the small sign for the Balkan Haus Restaurant. He contemplated how he wanted to deal with this man. Jake knew that if he came across too harsh the man would shut down out of pride and spite. After all, the man had once been an officer in the former Yugoslav Army, before morphing into the Serbian Army. Vesna Banduka had never been linked to war crimes like so many others from the Balkan War, but Jake knew that he had probably filtered a lot of money out of those countries—at least enough to start his restaurant.

As Jake got closer to the restaurant, he unzipped his leather jacket a little more and kept his eyes open for any possible danger.

In the past, Banduka had at least two men standing by out front, but there were no men in view tonight.

Jake went inside and the locals all turned to check him out. But the place seemed to have lost whatever charm it had back in the day, and only a few people were eating. More sat at the bar drinking beer, and some of these could have been Banduka's men.

Moving to the end of the bar, Jake ordered a beer and waited as he assessed those at the bar. Most looked to be older, in their fifties, except for one man at the far end who was perhaps thirty. And this man took a special interest in Jake.

Once Jake's beer came, he paid and look a long sip, ignoring the others at the bar.

The bartender wiped off some moisture close to Jake, so he took the opportunity to ask the man in German, "Does Vesna Banduka still own this place?"

The bartender's eyes shifted toward some of the others at the bar. Finally, he said, "Who wants to know?"

"I do."

"And you are?"

"Tell him Jake Adams wants a word with him."

The bar was small enough for everyone sitting there to hear their conversation. When Jake said his real name, a couple of them shifted their glance at Jake, including the younger man.

Without saying a word, the bartender left to a back room.

The young man finished his beer and came around toward Jake. Something was familiar about him, but Jake wasn't entirely sure who he might be.

The man stopped a bit too close to Jake and asked, "You are Jake Adams?" His English, infused with a Slavic accent, wasn't perfect.

Turning to the young man, Jake said, "Who the fuck are you?" As he kept his eye on the younger man, Jake assessed potential strike-points.

The guy went through a series of Serbian swear words, which were the only thing Jake understood in that language.

Then, as the young man wound up to swing his thick fist at him, Jake snapped a quick back fist with his middle knuckle catching the youngster solidly in the throat. The strike wasn't enough to collapse the man's trachea, but sturdy enough to put the man on his knees gasping for air.

"Jake Adams," came a voice from the back entrance. "Please do not permanently damage my nephew."

Jake glanced back and saw Vesna Banduka, or a reasonable facsimile of the man. The man had aged, and not so much chronologically as through the horror of disease. This once tall, strong man was now hunched over, gray, and leaning on a wooden cane.

Banduka shifted his head toward the back room and started shuffling off.

Yeah, the guy could barely walk. But Jake followed closely, keeping his eyes open for others at the bar who might follow them. None did.

Once inside his back office, Banduka settled gently into an old wooden swivel desk chair. A blow-up donut squeaked as he sat his decimated frame.

Jake stood out in front of the man's desk, showing as much deference to the old man as possible.

"Please, sit," Banduka said. "But before you do, could you pour me another glass of Scotch? Pour yourself one as well."

He wasn't a huge Scotch drinker. But this was 18-year-old Glenlivet, and cost about a hundred bucks a fifth. So, Jake poured them each a healthy dose of medicine before taking his seat across from the old Serbian Army officer.

"What kind of cancer?" Jake asked.

"Take your pick," Banduka said, and then took a sip of his single malt. "Started in the ass and spread to every inch of my body."

Hell of a way to go, Jake thought. "Sorry to hear that."

The old guy shrugged. "I should have been dead twenty years ago during that damn war. Anything after that was easy time." Banduka hesitated long enough to sip more Scotch and size up Jake with expressive eyes. "I'll have to let my nephew know that he almost got his ass kicked by a legend in the spy game."

"Maybe it will keep him alive a little longer," Jake said, and then tried his Scotch for the first time. He imagined it was exquisite, but he still preferred a good aged rum. "You might tell him that we got this gray hair by sticking around long enough to know some shit."

Banduka smiled and his frail body squeaked as if he had let out a fart. But it was probably just the blow-up donut. "What do they say in English? He's dumber than a box of rocks. I never did understand some of the English idioms."

The two of them stared at each other for a moment, with each taking a long sip of their drinks. Jake liked to let these awkward meetings play out in time, without an obvious flow. Although Banduka had a Slavic slur to his words, his English was nearly flawless due to his education in Scotland.

"I can imagine why you are here," Banduka said.

Jake said nothing. Let the man guess, he thought.

"This has to do with the disappearance of Anica Senka," Banduka said.

Jake tried not to respond non-verbally. Then he said, "You remember her?"

"Of course. What happened to her family was a tragedy."

"I appreciate your help in the matter back then," Jake said.

"I did nothing, Jake. It was all you."

Not entirely true. Jake was sure that Banduka had been responsible for the mysterious disappearance of Anica's relative. The one who had tried to rape the young woman. Although Jake had beaten the man senseless and turned him over to the local Polizei, somehow the man had been released under a strange bail system. Then the guy had probably ended up in the bottom of the Inn River.

Jake finished his drink and set the cup on the edge of the large wooden desk. He needed to get to the point, but he didn't want to rush a dying man.

"Please pour more," Banduka said. "This could be my last bottle."

The man was probably close to telling the truth, so Jake poured more for the both of them. Then he settled back into his chair and said, "Why do you think I'm here about Anica?"

"Because she came to me last week," Banduka explained. "She has transformed from a skinny little kid into a stunning beauty."

"And what did she want from you?"

"The same thing you probably want. But at the time I didn't give it to her."

"Yeah. What was that?"

"A name."

"Of who?"

"You have to understand, Jake. Things have changed in Innsbruck."

He had an idea where this might be going. "Why didn't you help her?"

"I did. I gave her the name of a contact who might be able to help her."

"Bogdan Maravich," Jake said.

"Yes. The man killed on the bridge with her that night. Before she went into the river."

"That's some help you gave her," Jake said callously.

"She was Polizei."

"Is Polizei."

"Right." The old Serb hesitated long enough to suck down a healthy dose of his medicinal Scotch. Then he said, "I had no idea there was a hit going down. You have to understand that things have changed here."

"Stop telling me that it has changed and tell me how it's changed," Jake said.

The old Serb's head flopped up and down like a bobble head, as if his neck wasn't strong enough to hold up his skull. "They are brutal. With no honor."

Jake thought the same could have been said about the old Balkan officers who escaped or survived that war. "Who are they?"

"After I put Anica in touch with Bogdan Maravich, and what happened on that bridge, I had my people look into the situation." The old guy, nearly out of breath, tried to pull some oxygen from Scotch.

"And what did they find?" Jake asked.

"Anica was on to something," Banduka said. "It's not just Serbs involved. It's a consortium of bad guys. The newly arrived."

"From the immigrant community?"

Banduka nodded his head. "I don't know who runs it, what they are into, or how widespread this goes."

"But Anica was obviously on to something," Jake surmised.

"Yes. The Austrian government is like most of the other governments in Europe. They are finally coming to the realization that they have made a mistake letting people into their country. People they can't possibly scrutinize properly. Refugee status used to mean something. Not anymore. People have been let into these countries who should have been thrown in jail. Many were in jail. And these dictators emptied their cells, shoved healthy young men onto boats, and gave them a one-way ticket to Italy or Greece. Then those countries mostly had enough sense to give them a one-way bus ride north."

Jake knew all too well about that practice. He had seen it happen first-hand in Italy when he lived in Calabria. Was that what this was all about? "What can you give me? Anything at all that can help me find Anica."

Trying to catch his breath with more Scotch, Banduka finally said, "Look into a man named Zoran Petrovic. A former Serbian soldier. A sergeant."

"Is he from Innsbruck?" Jake asked.

"He used to be here. But he is wanted for a number of crimes and has moved to Strasbourg."

Crap. This could be serious, Jake thought. Strasbourg, France was a cesspool of radical assholes. "You don't happen to have an address."

"Afraid not."

Jake finished his drink and set his glass onto the desk again. Then he got up and started for the door, but was stopped when the old Serb called to him.

"Jake."

Turning, Jake said, "I'm sorry. Thank you for the information."

The old guy smiled. "No, I was just going to say that the Tirol Polizei have a term in their crime statistics named after you."

He waited for the punchline.

"The Adams Affect," Banduka explained. "You see, since you left, violent crime in the city has gone down significantly. Now you are back and people are shooting up the streets again. Maybe you should stay away for the good of all Innsbruckers."

Jake simply smiled and left the dying man to himself. He walked out and got a wide birth from those men at the bar, including the man who had gotten struck in the throat.

He wandered down the street toward their car near the main train station, thinking about what he had just been told. Under normal conditions, Jake wouldn't have taken the old Serb's word for it, but the guy was dying and Jake didn't think he was lying. He took out his phone and typed in the name Zoran Petrovic to a contact of his within the Carlos Gomez organization. This man was a former officer with INTERPOL. If anyone had anything on Petrovic, this guy would know about it. Now he had to decide who else he would give this name. If anyone.

5

Strasbourg, France

Anica Senka was alone and confused in this French city on the edge of Germany on the west bank of the Rhine River. She wandered through the square in front of the Strasbourg Cathedral, where the sound of drums beating blended with the cacophony of protest chants from the seemingly disenchanted youth who blended with the newly arrived rabble.

It was nearly ten p.m. She had gotten to Strasbourg two days ago, after traveling from Innsbruck.

An old friend had let her use her older Passat, which had no GPS tracking on-board. Earlier that evening her phone had signaled her that someone was in her apartment, which sent a live video to her smartphone and saved a copy into the cloud. That turned out to be Johann Gruber, her old partner. She still wasn't sure what had gone wrong with her comm that night on the Innbrucke Bridge, forcing her to jump into the freezing waters of the Inn River. It was only by luck that she had not died of exposure that night. Then, shortly after Johann had gotten to her apartment, the motion sensor had gone off again. And this time an old friend had appeared in her apartment—Jake Adams. Uncle Jake, as she called him. What was he doing there? Maybe she could ask him some day.

But now she was on the hunt for the next link in what she was referring to as the chain of assholes. First, she had talked with the old dying Serb, Vesna Banduka, who had been less than totally helpful. At least the man had put her in contact with Bogdan Maravich. This man had lost his life in front of her, but not before giving her the name of Zoran Petrovic. This man had not been easy to find, considering he was on the run from the Austrian Polizei and had an INTERPOL Red Notice out on him.

Petrovic was like a cockroach. Which had made it easier for her to find him. Cockroaches lived in the dark, damp recesses of society. And Strasbourg was the perfect breeding ground for those types.

She had to believe that she could be walking into a trap, but that didn't bother her. Anica had put herself in this position, agreeing to work undercover for her organization and Europol. In the past couple of days, she had been able to research the background of Zoran Petrovic. After a short military career, where he had not officially distinguished himself in any significant way, he had emigrated to Austria during the open-border years, where nearly anyone with a pulse had been let in to her country. She knew that she could not be entirely critical of that policy, since it had also allowed her to come to Austria as a young refugee. But she had assimilated properly, excelling in school and finding her way into the Polizei. Petrovic, on the other hand, had gone in another direction, getting involved in petty crime, which eventually led to more serious larceny, robbery and assault. If she didn't need him to move up the rung of assholes, she would slap cuffs on the shithead and haul his ass back to Innsbruck. Unfortunately, she needed this man.

Anica had a feeling the man would not be alone, and she saw that her assumption was correct as Petrovic strut across the wide square as if he owned every stone beneath his feet. Two other men followed behind him, and one slipped around behind Anica when the three of them got closer. Petrovic was smoking a cigarette, blowing smoke into the night air in a grand gesture of superiority.

The man was easy to identify from his photograph in the Europol files. Petrovic had only one good eye, his right one. The left eye was glass, the shade of blue not even close to the dull gray of his right eye. His two men could have been locals, but they also had Slavic features.

"You are the woman from Innsbruck," Petrovic said in German.

The only way Anica could even get a meeting with this man was to impress him in some way. Petrovic obviously knew about the shooting of her contact that night on the Innbrucke Bridge. So, she had used that to her advantage.

"I need to know why your people killed Bogdan," she said.

"Was he a friend of yours?" Petrovic asked, his good eye undressing her from top to bottom.

She shrugged and moved a bit to her right to make Petrovic turn his head to see her completely. It also let her see the man behind her in her peripheral vision.

"I don't give a shit about Bogdan," she said. "He gave me your name just before he was killed. I was just curious why you killed your own man."

Petrovic shook his head and she thought the man's fake eye might drop out. "Bogdan was a weak man. Hardly a man at all. He was stealing money from our people."

"Your people?" she asked.

He seemed to pull back somewhat and bit his lip, as if he had said more than he should have, considering the fact that he might not have fully vetted Anica. How could he? Although she was using her real first name, she had taken on the surname Adler.

Petrovic lit another cigarette and flicked the last of his butt to the stone surface. "We are not all Serbs, if that's what you think."

In her background legend, she had used her Serbian as a hook to get her in. Which might have been a mistake. But it was a calculated choice.

In Serbian, Anica said, "I don't give a shit if I work only with Serbs. But I will not work with Muslims."

Petrovic and his two men laughed at that notion. "That goes without saying, Anica. We should have killed all those bastards during the war. Now they have infested Europe from the Middle East to Africa and even the Balkan states."

Now came her most important acting job, since she had several friends who were Muslim. Good people who were being lumped in the same category by a few radical jihadists. "I have no use for them either," she said, sticking to her native Serbian.

Petrovic made an approving face, as his head went up and down. "What do you want from me?"

"You are wanted by the Austrian Polizei and INTERPOL," she said. "Perhaps you could use my help in your organization." She had no idea of the full complexity of what these people did, but her briefing had mentioned they were into everything from international drug trafficking to human exploitation.

Petrovic laughed and then with derision said, "What can a girl possibly do for us?"

The man in Anica's peripheral vision started moving toward her. She considered drawing her weapon, but instead simply waited to see what he had planned for her. When the man reached for her left shoulder, she swiveled her body, grasped the man's hand and twisted it back, snapped a kick into the man's right knee and buckling him in pain.

Feeling the approach of the second man, still holding onto the first man's wrist, she spun around with a high kick, catching the second man with the toe of her boot in the left side of the man's face, dropping him to the solid surface. With the twisting of the first man's arm, he was screaming in pain now.

"All right," Petrovic said in Serbian. "Do not rip his arm off."

Anica considered a knee to the man's face, but instead simply took her boot and shove the man onto his back, where he tried to shake feeling back into his limb.

"So, you know how to handle a couple of men," Petrovic said. "I can hire muscle at any time. Look around this square. It's full of young men who are out of work."

Anica took off her hat, brushed her hands through her thick, dark hair, and put her hat back on again. A delay tactic. She knew she needed to play this just right, offering only the services she would be willing to provide to this man.

Finally, she said, "I can offer you more than my ability to kick ass on some thugs at your side."

"What is more important than protection?" Petrovic wanted to know.

"Information," Anica said. "I have the ability to access every police and border patrol database in Europe. But not just that. I can also access their operational systems." She let that sink in.

The chain smoking Serb, lit number three from his butt and took in a deep breath, bringing the tip to a bright orange. "How can I believe that?"

"I found you." She quickly drew her Glock and aimed it at the Serb's head. "And I could put a bullet into your skull in one second. You would be dead before your body hits the stones."

Petrovic didn't flinch. He looked to be partially aroused. "Maybe we could have a place for you in our organization. Assuming you can prove to us you can get the information we need."

She was afraid this next test could be harder than beating up a couple of ill-prepared thugs. But with her access, she knew she could handle anything they needed. Her only problem would be preserving the integrity of the Austrian Polizei and Europol systems.

They left it like that. Anica watched as the three men wandered back across the wide square and rounded the corner past the Strasbourg Cathedral, the men she had fought occasionally turning to glare at her, as if they would never accept her in their old boys group.

Suddenly, her phone buzzed and she pulled it from her back pocket. This was her private phone, which had been turned off until recently. The text read, 'We need to talk.' It was from the only person she could never say no to—Jake Adams.

•

A lone man stood in shadows across the square, having watched the entire encounter between the three men and the woman. She was amazing, he thought. She moved with such grace and speed, as if she had choreographed the entire fight scene. What would she do next?

As his target checked her phone, he imagined the two of them sitting down for drinks. Even coffee. Just to be in her presence would be enough for him.

But he had work to do. Get to it, boy!

6

Innsbruck, Austria

Jake sat at a booth in the hotel bar, sipping a local beer, but wishing they had something more than Puerto Rican or communist rum.

He was still waiting for Anica Senka to text him back. He was also waiting to hear back from his team at the Spanish communications company, telling him where Anica's phone had last pinged.

When the woman entered the bar alone, as he had requested, he noticed a difference from their last meeting in The Azores. Then she was wearing practical shoes and slacks, with a sweater coving her vital organs. Now, she was letting everyone know what she had. Everything was on display, and it reminded Jake of the first time they had met years ago, when Sabine Bauer was simply a lower-level Polizei officer sleeping with her boss. She wore tight black stretch pants and a skin-hugging white blouse. High heels stretched her frame to nearly six feet. Out of place was an oversized black leather purse, which had to contain her gun, extra magazines, and perhaps communications devices. Her hair flowed naturally over her strong shoulders as she strolled across the room, every male head turning to catch a glimpse.

When she sat down across from Jake, he nearly heard the deflation of egos from the other men in the room.

"Glad you could make it," Jake said, reaching his hand across the table to shake with Sabine, which she did.

"I was on a date," she said.

"Oh. I thought that might be the new uniform for Austrian cops."

Before she could respond, the waiter came over and took her drink order. Sabine would also have a beer.

Once the man left, Sabine said, "I haven't worn the uniform for years. But I am still Polizei."

The implication came across loud and clear to Jake. This was a business beer and nothing more. Of course, she had also met Sirena in The Azores, and Sirena could look at another woman and make them believe that one false move could be their last.

The waiter came with her beer and Jake told the man to put in on his bill.

"A business expense?" Sabine asked.

"This is a private endeavor," he said.

"I see." She took a long sip of her beer and licked the foam from her top lip. "Perhaps you could tell me why people keep shooting up my streets."

Jake raised his hands in protest. "Hey, I was just walking down the street when some crazy assholes started firing at us. Is it not alright to defend myself?"

She considered him carefully, her eyes wandering over his torso. "It is illegal to carry a concealed handgun in Austria."

"You forget that you asked me to come here and find your missing officer," Jake said.

"I didn't expect you to shoot up a quiet neighborhood," she said.

"What would you have me do," Jake said, "point my finger at the bad guys and make shooting sounds?"

She smiled and sipped her beer again. "You are quite the charmer. I think I see what the women in your life see in you." Sabine hesitated, unsure of her direction. Then she said, "I've looked into you. The President of Austria conferred upon you the Great Golden Decoration with Star of Austria, the highest honor Austria bestows upon any civilian."

"That was years ago," he said.

"And I understand you are officially a Teutonic Knight."

"Well, I left my sword at home."

"I will give you a break," she said, "since I know that you still have a permit to carry a handgun in Austria."

Good to know, Jake thought. But he already knew the laws of Austria, where he even needed a permit to purchase 9mm ammo.

"However," Sabine said, "My guess is that your girlfriend does not have a permit in Austria."

"Well. My international driver's license might also be expired, along with my library card. What's your point?"

"I'm just saying." She left it like that, as if she wanted Jake to know that she held some control over Sirena.

Jake wasn't sure where this was going. "Do you want me to find Anica Senka? Or would you rather sit here and discuss the Austrian penal code?"

"The former," Sabine said. "But I also want you to know about the Jake Adams impact on the Tirol crime statistics. Since you moved away, violent crime has dropped significantly."

Shaking his head, Jake said, "The man killed on the bridge the other night had nothing to do with me. As you know, I was in The Azores at the time."

"Understood."

They stared at each other for a long moment, neither saying a word. In that silence, Jake's phone suddenly buzzed in his pants. Sabine heard it as well.

"Do you need to check that?" she asked.

"Probably not." Then he thought of a way to explain himself. "There's a saying in America: If you want to make an omelet, you have to break a few eggs."

"I've heard that here in Austria also," Sabine said.

"Strangely enough, when I get involved with a case, sometimes eggs get broken."

"People also," she said.

"Only those who deserve it."

His phone buzzed again, but he ignored it for now.

"You should really check on that. It could be important."

Unfortunately, he had to agree with her, since he was waiting to hear back from Anica. Jake pulled his phone out, and saw over the top of his phone that Sabine had ordered them each another beer. The first text was not from Anica. It was from his private contact, who said he had a location for Anica. He shook his head when he saw where she was, and then moved on to the actual text from Anica. Her text read, 'Stay out of this, Uncle Jake.'

Interesting. That sounded more like a challenge than an order. He typed back quickly, 'All right.' But that was a lie, of course.

"You found her," Sabine said. "I can tell by the look on your face."

Maybe this Polizei officer had done more than sleep her way to the top. "More or less. A general area."

"But she's alive, right?"

The two beers came and the rather inattentive young waiter simply scurried away.

"She's alive," Jake said. "But I think she might be in trouble."

Sabine lifted her glass of beer and waited for Jake to do the same. They ticked their glasses together and each said *"Prosit."* Then they took healthy drinks from the new beer.

"Now what?" the Polizei officer asked.

"Now, I do what you asked me to do. I go get Anica."

"Maybe I should go with you."

"Not necessary," he said.

"My credentials could open some doors."

"Not where I'm going."

She raised her brows expressively. "She's not in Austria?"

He shook his head.

"Then where?"

"It's better that you don't know."

"Why?"

"Sometimes I'm required to do things that Polizei officers might find a bit. . ." How could he say this without pissing her off? "A bit questionable."

She drank more beer and had a look of interest on her face. He had obviously done more to entice than dissuade.

"You should at least take Johann Gruber with you," Sabine said.

"Why?"

"Because, like Anica, he has credentials he can use throughout the European Union."

Jake knew she had a point, but he didn't like the idea of babysitting. "When the bullets started flying tonight, Johann didn't even draw his weapon."

"Sounds like he could use your guidance," she said.

Or some balls, Jake thought. But he agreed to take the Austrian Polizei officer with him, knowing that she only wanted the young man with Jake so he could report back their actions to her.

Sabine pounded the last of her beer like a *putzfrau* after a grueling day cleaning up after Octoberfest drunks. Then she shook Jake's hand before leaving him alone at his table.

Jake watched as the men in the bar nearly got whiplash checking out Sabine's ass as she departed.

Seconds later, Sirena came in and again the sausage fest craned for a look at her. By Jake's thinking, Sirena was at least twice as hot as the Polizei officer, with her exotic darker features.

She sat in the chair Sabine had just vacated, waving for the waiter to bring her a beer.

"Well?" Sirena asked. "How'd it go?"

"Did you take care of business?"

"Roger that."

"Awesome. But we have a problem. I just got word that Zoran Petrovic is not the only one in Strasbourg. Our people tracked Anica there as well."

The waiter came over and set a beer down in front of Sirena and hurried off again.

She sipped her beer and then said, "We should get going then."

"We'll sleep a few hours and then get on the road," Jake said. "Did you tuck in Johann?"

"Are you sure you want him going with us?" she asked.

"Yep. And as suspected, Sabine just offered up his services to us."

"Has anyone ever told you that you should do this for a living?"

"Shut up and drink your beer."

7

Strasbourg, France

Jake rode with Johann Gruber in his Audi from Innsbruck to this French city on the German border, while Sirena drove behind them in a rental BMW. Jake needed to conduct a soft interrogation on the Austrian man, something Jake accomplished quite well. He knew that people liked to talk about themselves, yet many people never got the chance to divulge personal information because of the self-centered nature of many. Folks could be terrible listeners. But Jake had a way of asking people simple questions that would elicit desired answers, unfiltered and truthful. And the best part was that the one being questioned had no idea they were falling right into Jake's plan.

With Johann, though, Jake wasn't trying to grasp intelligence information. He was more interested in motivation and loyalties.

What did Jake discover? Nearly everything about the man's upbringing in rural Tirol. He had done some time in the Austrian Army prior to joining the Polizei. And the most important tidbit of information? Jake was certain that Johann had a crush on Anica Senka. Johann didn't just want to find Anica for professional reasons. He was truly concerned for her because he thought they might be able to get together at some point.

The trip from Innsbruck, Austria to Strasbourg, France was nearly 500 kilometers. With traffic problems and stops, they had made the trip in five hours.

Now, they drove slowly through the outskirts of the city, heading toward the city center. For some reason, the traffic had stalled up ahead and they were bumper to bumper.

"I don't know what's going on up ahead," Johann said, becoming frustrated.

Jake checked his watch. It was nearly three p.m. "We'll check into our hotel and rest before heading out."

"Are you sure you don't want to get the early-bird special at the hotel restaurant?" Johann asked.

"You watch too much American T.V."

"You are getting up there in age."

"I'll combine a few American idioms for you," Jake said. "Don't judge a book by his silver lining."

"I think that translates to German," Johann admitted.

Jake continued, "In this game, experience can keep you alive. If you want to be sharp tonight, you need to get some rest. Look in the mirror. Your eyes are red as beets. Five hours doesn't seem like a long drive, but on the Autobahn your eyes get overworked constantly shifting and looking for danger."

"Point taken," Johann said. The Austrian actually looked into his mirror now to confirm what Jake was saying. Then he added, "Tell me about Sirena."

"What about her?"

"The two of you are together obviously. How did that happen?"

"You mean how did an old guy like me score a hot Israeli like her?"

Johann glanced at Jake quickly. "I didn't know she was Israeli. She doesn't have much of an accent."

"That's because her mother was American," Jake said. "Plus, she speaks about a dozen languages. Never underestimate her." Jake made sure not to tell this Austrian Polizei officer that Sirena had once been an officer in the Israeli Army and had worked for the NSA, the CIA and on loan to the FBI several times, before retiring and coming to work with Jake.

"She looks at me like she wants to snap my neck," Johann said.

"It's nothing personal," Jake said. "I get that same look from her sometimes. Just remember that she could actually do it."

"Seriously?"

Jake shrugged.

Johann looked scared now. "Here we go."

They got through the gauntlet. The jam turned out to be a simple fender bender, bringing traffic to one lane. Once they got through, they had clear sailing all the way to their hotel in downtown Strasbourg, just a few blocks from the famous cathedral.

Jake and Sirena checked into one room, and Johann was just a couple of doors down from them.

They agreed to meet at seven for dinner before they headed out to try to find the Serb.

Once they got to their room, Sirena plopped down on their bed and let out a heavy breath.

Jake went to the window and viewed the city center. From their room, he could look down on the cathedral square a couple of blocks away.

Sirena propped herself up on her elbows and said, "What did you learn from Johann on the drive?"

Turning, Jake asked, "What do you mean?"

"You know what I mean," she said. "You could make a monk break his vow of silence."

"Yeah, well you could break any vow of celibacy."

"Thank you." She patted the bed. "Why don't you join me?"

How could he say no to her?

Afterwards, they took a long nap. Jake woke and found the room semi-dark. Sirena sat in a chair across the room checking her phone for something.

"Anything important?" Jake asked.

"Checking to see where Sabine was."

"And?"

"And she's still in Innsbruck," Sirena said. "At least her car is. What made you think she would follow us?"

"I don't know. She seemed to have more of a stake in finding Anica than she wants us to know. Why else would she fly all the way out to The Azores to hire us?"

"Because you're the best in the business," she concluded.

Jake got out of bed, still naked, and found his underwear, slipping them on. Then he put on black jeans and a dark gray T-shirt. Finally, he grabbed his socks and shoes and sat on a chair next to Sirena. "You have to admit that Sabine seems more invested."

"Maybe she had the hots for you back in the day."

"I don't think so. In fact, I think she didn't like me much. I made her old boyfriend look like a total tool on more than one occasion."

"That's because you were aligned with his predecessor, Franz Martini."

"Perhaps." Jake took out his phone now and pulled up a tracking app to see where Anica was right now. Damn it!

"What's up?" Sirena asked.

"She must have taken out her battery."

"You taught her well, Obi-Wan."

Jake's phone buzzed and he pulled it from his pocket. It was a text from his contact in the Gomez organization.

"Important?" Sirena asked.

"They tracked the current location of Zoran Petrovic," Jake said. "He's in an apartment complex about three blocks from here."

Sirena got up and said, "Let's go get him."

"He'll have friends."

"We have Johann."

True. But Jake also saw how Johann reacted last time someone started shooting at them. "Let's hope he doesn't freeze this time."

Jake and Sirena went to get Johann down the hall from their room.

"Let's go," Jake said, walking right into the Austrian's room and checking out the television show playing. "Seriously? Cartoons?"

Johann complained with both hands. "You don't understand. It's good and funny."

Jake let out a quick breath of air. "Okay. We'll talk later about this. For now, we have a location for the Serb."

"Wonderful," Johann said, and then found the remote control and turned off the T.V.

The Austrian started for the door, but Jake stopped him with his hand on the man's chest. "Are you forgetting something?"

Johann looked confused.

"Your gun," Jake said. "On the night stand."

The Austrian Polizei officer slapped his head. "Sorry. I must be more tired from the drive than I thought."

"I told you to take a nap," Jake instructed, like a disturbed parent.

Before leaving the room, Sirena set up everyone with comm earbuds, and they all did a quick check to make sure they were all on and reading each other.

Then they left the hotel. Jake and Johann walked down the sidewalk together, while Sirena went around to the parking garage to pick up the rental BMW.

"What's the plan?" Johann asked Jake.

"We're just going in to have a talk with the man. But remember that these guys are dangerous and probably heavily armed."

"I should arrest Zoran Petrovic," Johann said. "He is wanted by both Austrian Polizei and INTERPOL."

Jake stopped the young officer and said, "Let's hold off slapping the cuffs on the guy until we get the info we need."

Johann shook his head. "Damn it. I left my handcuffs in my bag at the hotel."

"Don't worry about it."

"You see, I haven't been in plain clothes that long. I used to have all of this gear on my service belt. I'm a bit lost without that."

"At least you have your gun and extra magazines," Jake concluded.

Johann cocked his head to the side. "I didn't bring extra magazines."

"I have two extra mags," Jake said. "And we both have the same Glock. We'll be fine."

They continued down the sidewalk. Darkness was now shrouding this French city. Jake noticed that a number of street lights had been either shot out or hit with rocks.

"Coming up behind you," Sirena said through the comm. "I'll be right out here."

As Jake turned to enter the apartment building, he caught Sirena parked in the BMW a block back, the engine still running.

Before heading up the stairs to the first level, Jake hesitated in the lobby and whispered to Johann, "Don't draw your weapon until I do. And then don't shoot me in the back."

"I have done this before," Johann said.

Right. "Just a reminder."

The two of them climbed the stairs and entered the corridor. Jake checked the door numbers and saw that the apartment would be about midway down the hallway. He guessed this place was probably a pretty nice place a couple of decades ago, before the anarchists started hanging out in Strasbourg.

"Moving in," Jake said, letting Sirena know where they were.

Jake had considered nearly every possible approach in situations like this—from kicking in the door to simply knocking and talking. This time, considering his back up, he would try the latter.

With a light knock, Jake backed up and smiled for those behind the door.

When the door opened, a plume of smoke billowed out into the hallway. Behind the smoke was a man in his early thirties. A man with definite Slavic features. But this was not Zoran Petrovic.

Jake considered a language, and he settled on German, since he knew Petrovic had lived in Austria for years. "I need to speak with Zoran," he said.

The man said something in Serb and started to close the door. "Tell him Jake Adams is here."

The man closed the door but Jake didn't hear it lock. He figured Zoran Petrovic would know his name and it might mean something to him. Jake could hear men arguing in Serbian behind the door. Arguments had no language barrier.

When the door opened again, it was the same man, a bit defeated. He shifted his head for Jake to enter.

"Wait here," Jake said to Johann.

"Are you sure?"

Jake nodded and entered what could only be described as a cross between a 50s Jazz club and a hookah den, right down to the red velvet sofa and chairs and subdued lighting. Standing across the room with a cigarette in one hand and a handgun in the other, was Zoran Petrovic.

"Holy shit," Petrovic said in English. "It is the great Jake Adams. I thought you would be dead by now."

"Me too," Jake said. "Can we speak without these two assholes?"

Petrovic's good eye shifted around the room at his men. In Serbian, the man told his men to leave. But instead of going to some back room, they went out into the hallway with Johann.

Once they were gone, Jake said, "Could you put down the gun?"

"Are you alright?" Sirena asked in Jake's comm.

"Everything is fine here," Jake said, to both Sirena and Petrovic.

The Serb smiled, sat in one of the plush chairs, and set his gun on the coffee table. "What can I do for you?"

Jake remained standing, contemplating tactics. Finally, he said, "How do you know me?"

"I lived in Innsbruck for many years," Petrovic said. "Word got around about you."

A good reason to no longer live there, Jake thought. Although he loved the beauty of Innsbruck, in his business it didn't pay to stay in one place too long. "Don't believe everything you hear."

Petrovic smiled and nodded his head. Then he found a pack of cigarettes and lit up another one. He must have thought the air had cleared too much. It hadn't.

"What do you need from me?" Petrovic asked.

"Information," Jake said. Then he slowly drifted toward the door as if leaving, but instead turned the deadbolt.

Petrovic went for his gun, but Jake already had his drawn and pointed at the Serb.

"I wouldn't," Jake said. "This can go one of two ways. Easy or hard. You know my reputation. Do you think I might lie to you?"

Leaning back into his chair, Petrovic smiled. "Lie, yes. But if you say you will do something, you will do it. That's why I went for the gun."

Jake shrugged. Then he went over and collected the man's gun, setting it across the room on a window sill. "Now it won't be so tempting."

"What do you need to know?" Petrovic asked, defeat in his words.

Trying to be careful with his words, so he didn't give away anything he didn't intend, Jake said, "Someone recently killed a friend of mine. I hear the killer was a woman with dark hair. Very pretty, but also capable of kicking some ass. I understand she might have offered her services to you recently."

"What do you want with this woman?" Petrovic asked.

"I want to make her pay," Jake said, hoping he wasn't burning Anica's cover.

"Maybe she is protected now. Did this friend of yours have it coming?"

"All of us have it coming, and we'll eventually get what we deserve." He hesitated, as if he had just spoken the greatest truth in his life. Then he said, "I just want to talk with her."

Petrovic shook his head. "Jake Adams doesn't just talk with people. At least not from what I heard."

Jake had rarely used his real name while living in Austria. But once his name had been leaked and then rumors had gotten out about him. Most of what was leaked was total bullshit and hyperbole. So, naturally, Jake had used that to his advantage.

Waving his gun at the Serb, Jake said, "Get up."

Somewhat confused, Petrovic put out his cigarette and rose from his chair.

Jake holstered his gun as he approached the Serb. Then, without warning, Jake punched the man with a right cross into the guy's left jaw. Two things happened. The Serb fell back into his chair, and then, surprisingly, the man's fake eye popped out of the socket and hit the floor, rolling to Jake's feet.

"Shit," Jake said.

"What the hell was that for?" Petrovic complained, rubbing his jaw.

With his right foot, Jake tried to roll the man's glass eye on the plush carpet, but it wouldn't move. It simply stared up at Jake.

"For not telling me what I'm going to ask you," Jake said.

"How did you know I won't tell you?" the Serb asked.

"I just assumed. It's like at a restaurant. You don't give a waiter a tip until you assure they deserve it. I'm turning things around. I gave you the tip, now you give me the service."

Petrovic seemed confused. "Okay. What is your question?"

"Where did you send the girl?" Jake asked.

The Serb put both hands up in protest. "Now, let's be reasonable. I can't just give you that."

"I know. That's why I smacked you. I wouldn't want your men to think you gave it up without a fight."

Now Petrovic seemed to register the concept. He stood up and came toward Jake, his hand out. "Give me my eye."

Jake punched the guy in the gut. Then he realized he needed to visibly damage the Serb, so he followed that up with several strikes to the guy's face, bringing instant blood from his nose and mouth. Petrovic hit the floor on his knees. Now Jake stepped back and let the Serb retrieve his glass eyeball.

Petrovic cocked his head back and popped his eye back into the socket. It was a little crooked, though.

Jake cocked his head to the side and twisted his fingers. "You're a little off."

The Serb adjusted his eyeball and got it almost right.

"Close enough," Jake said. "Now, tell me where the girl went."

"She works for us now," Petrovic said. "Which means she is protected by our people."

That's exactly what Jake wanted to hear. "I understand. I don't plan on killing her. I just need to ask her who paid her to kill my friend."

"I don't know anything about that."

"Where is she?"

The man hesitated, obviously wishing he had not sent his men to the hallway. "Riquewihr," he said painfully.

"Why?"

"She's meeting a man in our organization."

"Name."

Reluctantly, the man said, "Pierre Deval. He works at a winery in the old town."

"Jake, get out," Sirena said over his comm.

"Why?"

"Why does he work there?" Petrovic asked.

"No. Why did you send her to meet this Pierre Deval?"

"I can't say."

"Get out," Sirena repeated.

"All right," Jake said. "Thanks for the info."

Jake got to the door and was about to turn the dead bolt when he heard the first shots.

8

Sirena didn't like being left behind. In sports, that would be like leaving a star player on the bench. She had monitored the conversations of both Jake and Johann, who had not said much since Jake went into the apartment. She only picked up the dull ramblings of a couple of Serbs with Johann in the hallway. But then she saw the other man enter the apartment building, and something didn't seem right. That lone man was followed by two others. So, she had followed these men up to the second floor and simultaneously warned both Jake and Johann over her comm.

Once the shooting started, Sirena took up a position near the stairwell. From there she could peer around the corner and see that the doors down the corridor were all recessed a couple of feet, and men with guns seemed to be hiding in nearly every little nook.

There was screaming in French and German and Serbian, all of which she could understand. But the Serbian seemed to be a lot of slang.

"We've got a problem," Sirena said into her comm.

"No shit," Jake said. "I can't hear well from inside the apartment. What's going on out there?"

"One man down," she said.

•

Just after the shooting started, Jake heard a thud outside the door, the distinct sound of a body hitting the floor like a bag of potatoes. But which body? Was it one of the Serbs or Johann?

"Speak to me, Johann," Jake said.

"It's a mess out here," Johann said.

Good. At least Johann was alright, Jake thought. He turned and saw that Petrovic had retrieved his gun from the windowsill. Jake pointed his gun at the Serb. "I wouldn't do that."

"I'm protecting myself," Petrovic said.

"From who?"

The Serb shrugged. "I have enemies."

"Well, the police will be on their way."

Petrovic smiled, but Jake couldn't help smiling at the cockeyed nature of his glass eye, which now seemed to be looking hard to the left. Finally, the Serb said, "I have get out of jail free card in Strasbourg. Why do you think I live here?"

Jake shook his head and decided to act. With one motion, he unlocked the door and opened it quickly. One of Petrovic's men fell in, tripping over the other Serb, who looked dead. Dragging the man inside, Jake now saw Johann one door down and across the hall.

There was still yelling in French down the corridor. Then came screaming in German. Since Jake wasn't sure who these people were shooting at them, he decided he had only one choice—stay put. Besides, he knew that Sirena was down in the stairwell. She could get hit in the crossfire.

"Get in here," Jake yelled in English. Johann would have heard him through his comm and over the top of the other voices in German and French. "On my shots."

Reaching around the corner, Jake fired a few times high over the top, hitting the ceiling. But his shots gave Johann a chance to run toward him and slip into the apartment.

Johann slammed his body against a wall, his breathing hard.

"Are you alright?" Jake asked Johann.

"I think so."

"Who the hell are these people?" Jake asked.

"I don't know," Johann said. "It happened so fast. The first man came up and the Serbs pulled their guns. The man slipped into one of the doors. Then I saw the other two men, who started shooting. They shot this man. But something didn't seem right."

Sirens could be heard outside now.

"Sirena," Jake said. "Those men will be looking for an escape. Get out to the car."

"Are you sure?"

"Yeah. We can't afford to waste time with the French police."

"Alright. I'm gone," Sirena said.

Jake peered around the corner and saw the two men rush down the corridor toward the stairwell that led to the front door. Then a man stuck his head out partially, and Jake almost shot the guy. But at the last second, the man yelled 'Polizei.'

"Show me your badge," Jake said in German.

The man's hand rounded the corner holding a familiar leather case.

"Come closer," Jake demanded.

"How do I know you won't shoot me?" the man asked.

"The local police are outside," Sirena said over the comm. "You might want to get out."

"What about the other two shooters?" Jake asked Sirena.

"They slipped out just after me," she said.

Jake turned to Johann and said, "This is why you're with me. You'll need to show them your Polizei credentials."

Johann nodded. "Is that man German or Austrian Polizei?"

"Take a look."

Glancing around the corner, Johann said, "Rolf?"

"Johann?" the man in the corridor said.

"Wait," Jake said. "You know him?"

Before Johann could answer, the two men met out in the corridor, holstered their guns, and embraced. While the two men talked, Jake turned back to the apartment, where one man lay dead and the other was speaking to his boss, Zoran Petrovic.

"What's happening out there?" Jake asked Sirena.

"I don't know. The cops are just sitting there, not entering the building."

Turning to Petrovic, Jake asked, "Why aren't the police coming in?"

Petrovic came over to Jake and said, "They are afraid to come in. This is a sanctuary for many new people."

Afraid? What the hell! "Who were those people who shot your man?"

"How do they say this in English?" Petrovic fought for the right word. "Ingrates?"

"You mean immigrants."

"No. Well, they are that too. But they are not grateful for what they have here in Europe. We let them in and they don't assimilate."

"I understand that," Jake said. "But why kill your men specifically?"

"Competition," Petrovic said. "They want my business."

Jake wasn't sure what that business included, and he wasn't sure he needed to know. He was simply trying to bring an old friend back to safety. But, the closer he got to finding Anica Senka, the more he realized that she was working a case of her own—infiltrating this group. Had she gone rogue?

"Is there a back way out of this building?" Jake asked the Serbs.

"Of course," Petrovic said. "My man will bring you."

Now Jake felt a little bad that he had knocked the man's glass eye out of its socket. "Thank you."

Petrovic moved in closer to Jake. "Tell me you are not working for the Polizei."

"Anica is an old friend of mine from Innsbruck," Jake said. "I am like an uncle to her. Nothing more."

"But they are Polizei," the Serb said, shifting his head toward the hallway.

"Just during the day." He whispered into the man's ear now. "They want to have sex with Anica."

Petrovic smiled and nodded his head. "I understand the attraction."

Jake went out to the hallway and rounded up the Polizei men. "Let's go, boys."

"Wait," Johann said. "This is. . ."

But Jake cut the man off. "I said, let's go."

Petrovic's man brought them to a back corridor on the ground floor and instructed them to pass through the buildings to the side street.

As they walked, Jake told Sirena to bring the car around the block.

Finally, Johann caught up with Jake and stopped him by pulling on his arm. Jake looked down at the man's hand like he was about to rip the man's arm off and beat him with it.

"What?" Jake asked.

"I want you to meet Rolf Fischer," Johann said.

Jake shrugged as he looked over this man. Rolf looked like Shaggy from Scooby Do, right down to the hipster goatee and scrawny frame. "Were you two butt buddies back in the day?"

Johann looked confused and perhaps disgusted. "Do you have a problem with homosexuals?"

"I don't give two shits about who someone sleeps with," Jake said. "I'm just trying to establish relationships."

"Well, your gaydar is way off," Johann said. "Rolf has a girlfriend."

"We broke up," Rolf said, reaching his hand out to Jake.

Letting the man's hand hang for a second, Jake finally squeezed down and nearly crushed Rolf's skinny fingers.

They started walking again. Johann explained that Rolf was with Austrian Polizei. He had been with the State of Tirol division of Polizei, but transferred to Vienna a year ago.

"When Europol needed a liaison, I volunteered," Rolf said. "Just like Anica."

Jake stopped. "And how did you get here? More importantly, how did you almost fuck up Anica's cover?"

"I didn't mean to," Rolf said, like a hurt puppy. "I have been following Anica from Innsbruck. When she was nearly killed there, Europol sent me to find her."

Somewhat impressed that this man had been able to track anyone without Scooby snacks, Jake said, "So, Anica knows you are following her?"

Rolf shook his head. "No, sir. But I was watching her meeting with Petrovic last night. I lost Anica, but I was able to trace Petrovic and his men to this apartment building. I was ordered to simply watch and observe."

"Then why did you come in guns blazing?" Jake wanted to know.

"I didn't," Rolf pled. "The two men behind me started shooting. I didn't know if they were shooting at me or the Serbs. Who were those men?"

By now, Jake could see that Sirena had pulled the BMW to the corner ahead. He had half a mind to simply leave these neophytes behind and find Anica on his own. For some reason, though, he felt sorry for them.

As they walked to the car, the two Austrian Polizei officers argued about jurisdictional matters. While Rolf was working with Europol, he had authority in the European Union, with special dispensation with non-EU countries. Johann was also with Europol and the Tirol Austrian Polizei, yet his authority seemed to be somewhat limited to that country.

When they reached the car, Jake stopped and said, "Would you both shut the fuck up and get in the car."

Johann swished his hands together. "Where are we going?"

Jake shook his head. "To get our nails done. Where the fuck do you think? I've got a location for Anica."

Johann and Rolf both looked extremely happy as they piled into the back seat.

Getting into the front passenger seat, Jake stared straight ahead.

"Where to, boss?" Sirena asked.

Checking his watch, Jake realized it would be too late to drive to Riquewihr. That sleepy little wine town would be boarded up by the time they got there.

"We might as well go to the hotel and hit it hard in the morning," Jake said. Then he turned to the back seat and said, "Could you two stay in the same room without having a pillow fight?"

Rolf said, "This man is funny. I always heard that Jake Adams was an asshole."

"You heard right, Shaggy," Jake said. Then he leaned back and closed his eyes as Sirena pulled out toward their hotel a few blocks away.

9

Riquewihr, France

Anica Senka had spent the day driving from Strasbourg to the Alsace region on the border of Germany. Normally the drive would have taken an hour or so, but Anica had stopped frequently for coffee and a couple of wine tastings. This Riesling wine growing region had a difficult history, changing hands between the Germans and the French. Although the region was currently part of France, there were at least as many ethnic Germans living in Riquewihr and the surrounding hills of Alsace. Anica knew this from her school lessons, but she had seen firsthand the tension of those living here when she simply asked questions in the local shops earlier in the day. If she assumed they spoke German, and they were French, they would come off as cold and distant. Her French was not perfect, but the same would happen the other way around. Finally, she pretended to be American, speaking English with a southern accent. Now, both groups could hate her equally.

Earlier in the day she had finally found her target, a man named Pierre Deval, who was working in a small winery tasting room in the quaint old town of the city. She would have to admit that she was terrible at the seduction game. She couldn't even tell when a guy was trying to hit on her. So, she was clumsy at best trying to pick up a guy. And Pierre Deval didn't make it easy for her. It took Anica quite a while to even discover if he liked girls. Too many European men had become effeminate, and Pierre could have been the poster child for their movement. Pierre was a slim guy who looked like he was either on a hunger strike or was a strict vegan. He had one of those overly manicured skinny beards, and wore more eye under liner than Anica. Yeah, she would normally never even look at the man, let alone try to go out with him.

Now, after her tortured efforts, just an hour away from midnight, she wandered into a local pub looking for Pierre. The skinny hipster sat at a booth against the far wall, and he waved a couple of fingers at her.

As she crossed the bar, Anica caught a waiter and ordered a Czech pilsner. Then she took a seat across from the Frenchman.

"You found me," Pierre said.

"There aren't many bars open in the old town at this hour," she said, with a hint of disappointment.

"It's a tourist town," Pierre explained. "And not a fun one. This place is set up for old people who eat their dinner at four p.m. and go to bed by eight."

Anica's pilsner magically appeared and then the waiter slipped away like a ghost. She sipped her beer and licked her lips. A delay tactic. This man was hard to read. The only reason he had eventually agreed to this meeting was because she had name dropped, mentioning she had been told to come here by the Serb, Zoran Petrovic.

The Frenchman was on his phone typing something. More importantly, he was ignoring Anica.

"Didn't your mother teach you to not ignore a woman?" she asked.

Without looking up, Pierre said, "My mother is dead. So is my father."

"I'm sorry."

He shrugged. "Don't be. They were assholes."

This wasn't going as planned, she thought. She needed to move up the chain of this organization to understand the true nature of their business. But so far all she had run across were a bunch of thugs and a disengaged hipster.

"Zoran Petrovic," she said.

Pierre finally looked up from his phone. "What about him?"

"He sent me here."

"Who do you think I'm texting with?"

"Then he will confirm this."

Setting his phone on the table, Pierre said, "One of his men was shot tonight at his apartment."

"Is he alright?"

"The man is dead." Pierre hesitated, his gaze piercing into her eyes finally. "He said a friend of yours came by and struck him so hard it knocked his glass eye out."

Damn. "Is he sure this man knows me?"

"Positive. And he said the man is the most dangerous person he has ever encountered. A guy named Jake Adams."

Crap, she thought. Why was Uncle Jake involved? "I have been off the grid for a while," she said. "And he is like an uncle to me. He worries." Perhaps she could use Jake's reputation to influence this man, assuming Jake had kept her cover intact. Knowing Jake, he had enhanced her reputation.

"Petrovic said this man had an Austrian Polizei man with him. Are you Polizei?"

"Do I look like Polizei?"

Pierre shrugged.

"It could have been an old boyfriend," she lied. "You tell some people no so many times, you would think they would finally understand you are not interested."

"This Jake Adams fellow mentioned that the man wanted to have sex with you. I understand why. That makes sense."

She guessed that Johann Gruber had to be the man with Jake. But why had he come? Why did the Polizei allow it?

"Are we going to just talk?" Anica asked. "Or will you have sex with me?"

The Frenchman almost said something, but must have decided not to question fate like this. Instead, he put some money on the table paying for both of their beers, and then he got up to go. "Are you coming?" Pierre asked.

Anica got up. "That depends on your skill."

"I'm French. Need I say more?"

Pierre escorted her a couple of blocks to his apartment, which was on the second floor of the place where he worked—the winery tasting room.

Once inside, Anica said, "You have a short drive to work."

"This place is small, but it's part of my pay. Would you like some wine?"

She glanced at the bed and back to Pierre. "That sounds great. Riesling?"

"Of course." Pierre opened a bottle and poured them each a glass. He handed her one.

She took a sip and said, "I don't normally jump in bed with men."

"I must go to the bathroom," Pierre said, setting his glass of wine on the small kitchen table.

As soon as he went into the bathroom, Anica drugged his wine. Moments later, Pierre came out naked. The skinny guy had what could only be described as a micro-penis. She couldn't tell if it was hard or not, since it barely poked through his pubic hair.

"Wow. This is a surprise," she said. She sipped her wine, but couldn't keep her eyes off his tiny penis. "Have you considered getting into porn?" Child porn, perhaps.

"You are mocking me," he said, picking up his wine and taking a healthy drink. "I make up for my lack of stature with other techniques." He licked his lips with a massive tongue.

"I see," Anica said.

He smiled and finished his wine. Then he said, "Let's see your body."

She grabbed his little penis and pulled him toward the bed. Then she pushed him onto his back and his penis looked like a night crawler poking its head above thick grass.

"Before we do this," she said, "I must also go to the bathroom. Keep it ready for me."

He scooted his body up the bed, putting his head on his pillow while he stroked himself with two fingers, a smile on his face.

Anica went into the bathroom and ran the water. Since she was there, she peed. Then she flushed and checked her watch. That should be enough time, she thought.

Heading back to the main room, Anica said, "I hope you kept things going while I was away."

When she rounded the corner, she saw Pierre flat on his back. His penis was now as flaccid as linguini. In the morning, he would have to imagine what a stud he had been. Of course, she would be gone. But not before she took care of a couple of things.

First, she found Pierre's phone and accessed his call log. Then she ran through his recent text messages. She read the conversation Pierre just had with Zoran Petrovic. The Serb had in fact told the Frenchman about Jake Adams and associates. Petrovic had said some brutal things about Jake, but the Serb said he thought Jake might be working with the Polizei. Pierre asked what to do, and Petrovic said, 'Fuck her and kill her.'

Now she didn't feel bad about drugging that French asshole. In fact, she planned to do a couple of things to this man now. But first she needed to find out everything she could about their organization. She got onto the man's wireless and uploaded everything from his smart phone to a jump drive. Then, after turning on her smart phone, she transferred his data to her own phone. Next, she found his laptop. But, after an exhaustive search, she was sure there was nothing of importance on there.

Back on her phone, she pulled up Pierre's files and started to scan through them. She glanced across at the bed with the naked Frenchman. "You really screwed up, Pierre," she said aloud. A simple password would have made this much more difficult.

Suddenly, her phone buzzed and she looked to see who was calling. It simply said, 'Teutonic Knight,' which made Anica smile. She considered not answering it, but needed to know what he knew.

Taping on the answer button, she said, "Uncle Jake."

"It's about time you turned on your phone. How is Riquewihr?"

Ignoring his question, she said, "Why are you tracking me?"

"I need to know you're alright," Jake said.

"I'm fine."

"Well, don't trust the Frenchman, Pierre Deval."

How in the hell? "What makes you say that name?"

"Petrovic gave the man up too fast."

"I was thinking the same thing," she admitted, glancing at the naked man on the bed. "Pierre mentioned something about you knocking the eyeball out of Petrovic."

"An unfortunate incident," Jake admitted with a slight chuckle.

There was a momentary lull in their conversation.

Finally, reluctantly, she said, "I think I have a problem."

"That's why I'm here, Anica. You know that I'd do anything for you."

"I have Pierre's phone," she said. "He got a text from Petrovic saying to bed me and then kill me."

"Where's the Frenchman now?"

"Naked and in bed."

"You didn't."

"No, of course not. He's taking a long nap."

"Good girl. Can you get some intel out of him?"

"I've downloaded everything from his phone to mine. Do you think I should share the data with my people?"

"Polizei or Europol?"

"You know about my affiliation with Europol?"

"Yes. In fact, part of the incident tonight brought out a man who had also been tracking you. A guy named Rolf."

"Rolf Fischer?"

"Yeah."

"He's there with you?"

"Along with Johann Gruber and my friend Sirena."

"I heard that you had a new partner. Sorry to hear about Alexandra. I wish I had known at the time, but I didn't hear until months later."

"Thanks."

"Wait, you said Johann was there also?"

"Yes. Is that a problem?"

"Not at all. What do you think of him?"

"I think he's a little raw."

"He has not been introduced to the world of Jake Adams."

"What does that mean?" Jake asked.

"What do they say in America? Shit happens around your sphere of influence."

"When you poke a tiger, expect to get scratched."

She had to agree with that. But now she wasn't sure what to do with her current case. Was she burned? Probably. More than likely. Definitely.

"What should I do with this guy?" she asked.

"Do you have a knife?" Jake asked. "I'd cut his nuts off and make them into earrings. If you do that, send me a pic."

"I can't do that."

"He was going to kill you."

Jake had a point.

"Never mind," Jake said. "Put his clothes back on him."

"Do you know how hard it is to put clothes on a passed-out man?"

"Unfortunately, yes. Anyway, once you do that, then tie his ass up and wait for us to get there in the morning."

Anica agreed and then gave Jake the address for the Frenchman's apartment.

"I'll take care of that asshole," Jake said. "Get some sleep."

"It's about an hour's drive from Strasbourg to here," she said. "Forty-five minutes the way you drive."

"Funny. We'll get there early. Take care."

She shoved her phone into her back pocket and went to work on Pierre. This man was ready to use her and then kill her. He should have to pay for that intent. She smiled when she thought about what she should do to him. But in the end, she simply dressed the man, tied him up tight and strapped him to the headboard. It would be a long night, she thought. But this man would talk. Everyone talked.

10

Europol Headquarters
The Hauge, the Netherlands

It was nearly midnight, but Verner Kappel, Europol Deputy Director of Operations, was still in his office in the top level of the gray brick building center tower. Kappel was a former German Polizei officer who had retired from his home in Berlin to take this post with the European Union's law enforcement agency.

Now he was starting to question if he should have simply taken his Polizei retirement and settled into a country cottage on one of the lakes on the outskirts of Berlin.

Kappel was at his office for one reason. One of his deputies, the director of The European Migrant Smuggling Centre (EMSC), had called him and said they needed to meet on short notice. The Spaniard, Antonio Garcia, was new to the EMSC, so he was still trying to get a good grasp on the job. In fact, the EMSC was only a couple of years old. It was formed after the member nations saw a huge influx of migrants following wars in the Middle East and North Africa.

Standing at his narrow window overlooking the city lights, Kappel didn't turn when there was a slight knock at his door. Then he saw Garcia in the window's reflection, slip in carrying a tablet.

"Sir," Garcia said, stopping out in front of his desk.

Kappel turned and noticed that his deputy was wearing jeans and a T-shirt. It looked like he had just come from the bar down the street. By contrast, Kappel was still wearing his gray suit, although he had loosened his red tie somewhat.

"Please, s…sit," Kappel said. He took his seat and Garcia followed his lead, sitting down across from him. "Now, what could not wait until m…morning?"

"We have a problem in France," Garcia said, tapping his tablet.

"Explain."

"It's Anica Senka," Garcia said.

"The Austrian woman."

"Yes, sir. She was undercover in Innsbruck infiltrating a Serbian-run criminal operation."

Kappel had already been briefed on this as it happened. "Yes, I know. She was off the grid for a while."

"The other Austrian we sent to back her up has reported in," Garcia said.

"Rolf Fischer from Vienna."

"That's correct. Rolf said there was a shoot-out in Strasbourg tonight in an apartment complex between the Serbs and a couple of unknown assailants. He said he was nearly shot."

"Did anyone get hurt?" Kappel asked.

"One Serb was killed," Garcia said. "But we have another problem. Rolf said the Serbs were meeting at the time with an American. A former intelligence officer."

"CIA?"

"Yes, sir. He spent a lot of time in Germany, so I thought you might have come across him in the past. His name is Jake Adams."

Kappel shook his head, and tried his best to control his speech. "Never heard of him."

"After leaving the CIA, he was a prominent security consultant in Austria. He lectured at nearly every major security conference in Europe."

"Now that sounds familiar," Kappel said. "What was this man doing there?"

"Apparently, he's old friends with Anica Senka. Known her since she was a child. Somehow, he got wind that she was missing, and he started tracking her down. He's with an Israeli woman. Rolf thinks she was former Mossad."

Mother of God, Kappel thought. That's all they needed. "Has Anica checked in?"

"Yes, sir. She wasn't at the apartment during the shoot-out. By then, she had already gone to Riquewihr."

"Why Alsace? Other than good wine."

"To meet up with a wine merchant," Garcia said. "Anica thinks they might be smuggling migrants through wine routes. One more thing, sir."

Great. "What's that?"

"Well, two more things. First, the former intelligence officers also had a current Austrian Polizei officer with them. He's also affiliated with Europol."

"How is he involved?" Kappel asked.

"He's a former partner of Anica's. He also thought something might have happened to her."

"And, I'm guessing you saved the best for last," Kappel said mockingly.

"That's a matter of perspective, sir," Garcia said. "Anica got word that the French wine man was going to rape and kill her."

"What?" Kappel slammed his hands down on his desk.

"It's all right, sir. She got the upper hand and has the man in custody for interrogation."

Under normal circumstances of law enforcement, that was perfectly logical. But Europol was not a traditional police organization. They were mostly a coordinating agency with a building full of analysts connecting the dots among the EU member states. Kappel had made changes to that structure, though. Now, Europol officers were in the field gathering first-hand knowledge, instead of only sitting back and collecting the crumbs from state police. He wanted to make Europol more like INTERPOL. Even better.

"We do not have facilities for interrogation," Kappel explained to his deputy. "Did you ask Anica how she would accomplish this?"

"No, sir." Garcia shifted nervously in his chair, his right knee tapping up and down. "I thought it would be best if we both had plausible deniability."

Kappel had met Anica Senka only a couple of times. She always had an intense look in her eyes, as if she could choke him out for saying the wrong thing.

"Alright," Kappel said. "Tell her to carry on and report back with what she discovers."

Garcia nodded and realized he was being dismissed, so he got up and headed toward the door.

"Hang on," Kappel said. "Make sure you do a thorough background on those intel officers and the Austrian Polizei officer."

"Yes, sir. I'll get back with you as soon as I can."

Once his deputy was gone, Kappel got back up and glanced out the window again. Yeah, he didn't need this anymore. The European Union had no good reason to have a law enforcement agency. It was simply another level of oversight. Everything they did could simply be done by the member states, if they would simply talk with each other. That was the rub, he knew. On a personal level, he was proud of how he had been able to control his stammer.

11

Riquewihr, France

Jake rounded up his crew at dark thirty. Then they took two cars toward the south, making it to this small tourist town in the Alsace hills just as the sun was rising over Germany to the east.

Jake and Sirena got out of their rental BMW and walked back toward Johann and Rolf in their car.

Johann powered down the driver's side window. "It should be just two blocks down the side street and then left on the main tourist walk platz."

"Okay. We'll go in first. You guys hang back and watch our back out on the street."

"Will do. Is she answering her phone yet?"

Jake shook his head. "She must have turned it off again."

"Why would she do that?" Johann asked.

Grasping the side of the car, Jake glared in at Rolf. "I don't know. Do you have any idea, Shaggy?"

"Why does he keep calling me that?" Rolf asked Johann.

"It's obviously a term of endearment," Johann explained.

"I have no idea," Rolf said.

Somehow, Jake didn't believe the man. Despite that, he shifted his head for Sirena to move down the street with him toward the Frenchman's apartment.

"You're pretty hard on those men," Sirena said.

He knew that. "They need to toughen up. The shadow game isn't something you can play half-assed."

"I know. Just quit going so Jake Adams on their asses. Think of them like you would your son, Karl."

"I was pretty hard on Karl last time we were together," Jake said. "If they don't like how I'm treating them, they can go back to Austria and play with their Legos."

She slapped his butt and then took his arm, the happy couple wandering up the lane to get coffee and crescents.

The wine store had a recessed front entrance with two doors. One was a long glass door into the shop, and the one to the left was wooden and led to the apartment. It was just as Anica had described.

"She might have left it open for us," Sirena said.

Jake pushed down the lever and the door swung in. He shrugged and went inside, with Sirena right on his heels. When they got upstairs, another door was unlocked, so Jake simply went inside. The place was a small studio apartment with a kitchen area off to the right, a small living area just inside the door, and a bed up against the far wall. He saw immediately that Anica had been there, since there was a skinny man tied up and strapped to the bed. He was awake and struggling against his bindings. His mouth was taped shut over the top of a sock jammed down his throat.

The Frenchman's eyes were wide when he saw Jake and Sirena. He had been beaten up significantly, with his left eye nearly swollen shut. Blood had caked up around his nostrils, his mouth, his eyes, and his ears. And these were only the man's visible wounds.

"Check the bathroom," Jake said to Sirena.

She went off and came back in a couple of seconds. "Nope."

The man was trying to say something.

Jake sat on the edge of the bed and ripped the tape off the man's face, nearly extracting the man's skinny beard in the process. Then he pulled out the wet sock and dropped it on the man's chest.

The man said something quickly in French. Although Jake could understand much of his words, he asked the man to use either German or English.

Catching his breath, the Frenchman said, "This crazy woman tried to kill me. She just left moments ago."

"Seriously?" Jake asked. "That's the story you want tell?"

"It's the truth."

From memory, Jake said, "Pierre Deval. Thirty-two. French citizen. Lowlife douche bag. Wanted by INTERPOL for too many crimes to innumerate. And now you've gotten involved with a group of Serbs and others who will slit your throat if you tell me what I want to know."

Pulling out his Glock, Jake shoved the barrel into the man's forehead and continued, "But what you don't realize is that I don't give a shit. I work with people in the organization."

Pierre shook his head. "You are the police?"

Jake laughed. "You are Zoran Petrovic's little bitch. I'm from way up the food chain higher than that. Now, you have only one way to survive today. You tell me everything you told that woman."

Pierre tried to shake his head again. "I told her nothing."

"Then why are you still alive?" Jake asked. "That woman is a brutal murderer. She has worked for the Russians as a hit woman, leaving a trail of bodies across Europe. And you're telling me that she let you live?"

With this new information, Pierre started squealing like a wounded rabbit. He told Jake and Sirena everything he had told Anica.

"Are you sure that's everything?" Jake asked, tapping his gun barrel against the man's sweaty forehead.

"Yes, ja, si, oui," Pierre said.

Jake put his gun away and started toward the door.

"Wait. You must untie me."

Pulling Sirena aside, Jake whispered, "What should we do with this asshole?"

She looked over Jake's shoulder at the guy. "If we leave him, he will eventually get free. Now, he thinks you work for their organization. And you have enhanced the criminal reputation of Anica."

"But if we set him free and he talks with Zoran Petrovic, that could be a problem," Jake reasoned.

"She beat this man to get information," Sirena said. "If she was with the organization, she would already have this knowledge."

As usual, Sirena had a damn good point. Although Jake had tried to cover his tracks here, it wasn't clear if Anica had done the same for herself. "What if we have our Polizei friends take this man into custody? They could hold him for a while and keep him quiet."

"Rolf and Johann don't have jurisdiction in France."

"Not exactly true," Jake said. "Both are part of Europol, with authority to at least detain until the local police arrest the man."

Sirena shook her head. "The locals will see Pierre as a victim."

"Would you stop making so much sense?" Jake turned and studied the man for a moment. Turning back to Sirena, he said, "Alright. Find a new sock and bring the tape. We're taking him with us."

"To what end?"

"I'll figure that out later," Jake said. "We'll take him across the border into Germany and drop him off." Now, Jake turned to the Frenchman and said, "You're going to come with us and verify the information you just gave us."

"But I am telling you the truth," Pierre said.

"We'll see." Another reason not to let Pierre go, of course, was that he could call the man he had given up to Anica and that would put her in danger.

They washed Pierre up a bit and taped his hands behind his back. Now they could escort him to the car without drawing too much attention. They would have to keep him quiet, though. So, Sirena taped his mouth shut and then Jake covered his head with a brown pillowcase.

When they got downstairs, the two Austrian Polizei officers were told to stay quiet as they escorted the man to the cars. Jake shoved the guy into the back seat of the rental BMW and drove off, with Rolf and Johann pulling out behind them.

Once they got to an isolated location on the outskirts of town, Jake pulled over and got out. As he opened the back door, the Frenchman tried to kick Jake, but he missed terribly. Jake hauled the guy out and brought him around the back of the car. Then he popped the trunk and shoved the man inside. But Pierre slashed around like a fish in the bottom of a boat. Jake shook his head and simply punched the man in the face. Blood instantly started to soak through the pillowcase, but the man didn't move. Jake slammed the trunk and went back to speak with the Polizei officers.

"What are you going to do with this man?" Rolf asked.

"I don't know," Jake said. "Do you guys have a shovel."

"We can't kill him," Rolf pled.

"I was kidding. We'll take him into Germany and drop him off."

"That's kidnapping across borders," Johann said.

"What? No. We're just taking him for a ride."

"But what about the mask?" Rolf asked.

"He's sensitive to light."

"And the punch in the face?" Johann wanted to know.

Jake hesitated. "He said something about my dead mother."

"That wasn't nice," Johann concluded. "Where to now?"

"Germany. Follow me."

Jake went back to the BMW and sat behind the wheel, contemplating what to do. He wasn't sure keeping these two Austrian Polizei officer around was a smart play. He wasn't used to trying to justify his actions. And he had no idea what kind of Boy Scouts these two would end up being.

"Everything alright, Jake," Sirena asked.

"Yeah. I think so. You heard Pierre give up the information he had told Anica. Do you think he was telling me the truth?"

"About fifty percent chance," she said. "After all, you did have a gun to his head."

Jake turned over the engine and glanced back at the men in the car behind them. "I hate getting those two involved in this."

"Because you do things a little unorthodox?"

"I have trust issues," Jake said as he put the car in gear and pulled out onto the priority road.

"Really," she said with a smirk. "I never noticed that."

She noticed, he thought.

12

Konstanz, Germany

It took Anica Senka about three hours to travel from Riquewihr, France to this German city on the shore of Bodensee, or Lake Constance. Across the large lake was Switzerland. On a good, clear day, one could see the Alps to the south and east, but at mid-day on this day, Anica could barely see the lake, since heavy cloud cover enveloped the city and rain came down in a constant mist.

The Frenchman, Pierre Deval, had given her the name of a contact in the city. This was another Serb named Goran Goluža. After getting to Konstanz, she had turned her phone back on and used it to access the Europol criminal database to do a background on Goluža. Like many of the other Serbs she had come across, this man had once been in the military. But his records were sealed, which meant he had probably been in a special unit. Or, he had testified against those who had committed war crimes. As far as she could tell, Goluža owned a small trucking company. Which is how Pierre knew Goluža. He shipped the French Alsace wine for Pierre.

Late in the afternoon now, with no let-up in the relentless rain, Anica sat in her VW Passat and watched the small shipping platform that could accommodate four trucks. One truck sat idle and another was being unloaded into a small warehouse, which did not make sense to Anica. The Serb's company was supposed to simply pick up shipments at one location and drop them off elsewhere. It was possible that Goluža used the warehouse for temporary storage before consolidating shipments.

Suddenly her phone buzzed, startling her. She had forgotten to turn it off after researching the Serb.

Looking at the phone, she saw that it was from a place called *Easy Hands Massage Parlor*. She shook her head at the ingenuity of Jake Adams.

Finally, she tapped on to the call and said, "Does this massage come with a happy ending?"

"Let's just say that our customers always come first," Jake said.

"You will have to teach me that phone trick," Anica said.

"First," Jake said, "you need to tell me why you didn't wait for me in Riquewihr."

"I thought about that," she said. "I'm supposed to be undercover. We could not be together there. Did you find Pierre?"

"It was hard to miss him," Jake said. "Especially the way you left him."

"He was supposed to rape and kill me," she said. "If he had tried that, I would have been justified to defend myself and finish him."

"Understood," Jake said. "What did he give you? And where are you now?"

She hesitated way too long as she came up with her lie. "He didn't give me much." Anica knew that Jake would have tracked her GPS, so it wasn't like she could lie about her location.

"He must have given you something, Anica. Otherwise, why go to Germany?"

"Who did you tell Pierre you were?"

"I didn't tell him shit about me, other than the lie that I was with his organization and wanted to know what he had divulged to you."

Damn it. Now she could not lie to Jake. "What did you do with Pierre?"

"I should have put a bullet in his head," Jake said. "Nobody messes with my Anica."

She smiled with that sentiment. "I'm sorry I left, Uncle Jake. I didn't want to get you involved."

"It's a little late for that, girl."

Anica hesitated as she watched a man close the back of a large transport truck and lock it. Then she said, "You didn't let Pierre go."

Jake said, "Not exactly. He's still a little tied up. I didn't want him calling and warning anyone."

"Thank you."

"What are your plans?" he asked. "You can't take on Goran Goluža and his men on your own."

This man was incredible, she thought. Now he not only knew where she was, but he knew who she was currently tracking. "How?"

"As a Polizei officer, you have to follow certain rules," Jake said. "I'm not constrained in that way."

She mumbled a derogatory term under her breath in Serbian.

"Hey, I heard that."

"I'm sorry. I forgot that I taught you some bad words in Serbian."

"Yeah, and I'm still trying to figure out how a young girl knew those words."

The afternoon bells clanged in a nearby church. Funny thing, she heard them outside her car and also in the phone.

"Are you driving here?" Anica asked.

"Not exactly," Jake said. "I'm a couple of blocks back from you."

She looked into her rearview mirror and saw parking lights go on and off on a dark BMW.

"Let me help you," Jake said.

Did she have a choice now?

•

The drive from Riquewihr, France to Konstanz, Germany had been interrupted only a couple of times with banging from the trunk. Then Jake had been forced to get out, open the trunk, and tell the man to settle down or he'd get a bullet in the head.

Now, they sat back a couple of blocks from the VW Passat, and Jake had just told Anica that he should take the lead talking with Goran Goluža. She had reluctantly agreed.

"Are you sure this is a good idea?" Sirena asked Jake.

"The higher up the chain you get with these assholes the more dangerous they get," Jake said. "Anica should not go in there alone."

"I know that. I just have a bad feeling about this."

"Hand me an additional comm unit for Anica."

Sirena pulled a small plastic zip bag from the glove box and handed the ear bud to Jake. "Distress word is?"

"Posse," Jake said. "Make sure our Polizei friends know this as well."

"Roger that."

Jake got out into the light mist and watched Sirena slide behind the driver's seat. Then he shoved his hands in the pockets of his leather jacket, hoping the waterproofing he had put on the leather would hold up.

He got to Anica's car and slipped into the passenger seat.

Anica immediately gave him a strong hug, holding him tight to her body like a child who had been away from a parent for a long time. Then she pulled away a bit and kissed him on both cheeks. "I missed you, Uncle Jake." She wiped a tear from her right eye.

"I missed you, too, Anica. You look different."

"Older," she said.

"You'll always be that scrawny little kid who knocked on my door, tears in your eyes, asking me for help."

"Do you know how hard that was for me?"

"I can only imagine."

"I had watched you come and go for days," she said. "Always so serious looking. But you held the door for the old woman on the first floor and helped her with her packages. You always had a smile for me. So, I thought I was safe coming to you."

"In your circumstances, it must have been hard to trust anyone."

She nodded her head and wiped another tear away.

He pulled out the comm earbud and handed it to her.

"I have one," she said.

"One that failed you in Innsbruck," he said. "This one is much higher quality. You can use it under water."

Anica looked at the ear bud carefully. "This is only used by intelligence agencies. How did you get it?"

"I know a guy." He smiled at her.

"Never mind." She put the earbud into her right ear. "What's the range?"

"Infinite. It runs off your cell phone. All of us are on simultaneously. The best part is our communications are encrypted and stored. So, don't say anything you don't want hanging around in the cloud forever."

"Good to know," she said.

"Alright. You're live now. Comm check. Testing." He turned to Anica and said, "Our distress word is Posse. Acknowledge."

Sirena did so. Then the two Polizei officers also did so.

"Testing," Anica said. She gave Jake a thumbs-up.

Jake and Anica got out and headed toward the warehouse. The truck that had been unloading into the warehouse passed them and Jake memorized the license number, which he whispered into his comm unit.

"On it," Sirena said. "Better yet, Johann?"

"Passing us now," Johann said. "Swiss plates. I'll check on it."

They wandered side-by-side toward the door near the loading docks. Jake went in first and was immediately met by a group of desks. Only one was occupied by a pension-aged woman who looked like she could still throw boxes into the back of trucks.

"What can I do for you?" the woman asked in German.

"I am here to speak with Goran Goluža," Jake said.

"He is in the warehouse," the woman said, "but you cannot go in there."

"Could you get him for me?"

Reluctantly, the woman picked up an old flip phone and punched in a programmed number. Then she spoke into the cell phone in Serb.

Anica touched Jake's hand and the two of them exchanged a glance. Whispering into Jake's ear in English, Anica said, "She thinks we're cops."

Jake kissed her on the cheek and said, "You are."

The woman flipped her phone closed and set it precisely on her desk. "He will be here soon."

"I don't like this," Anica said.

"That makes two of us." Jake unzipped his jacket for better access to his Glock.

Jake half expected the Serb to come through the side door to the warehouse with a number of men pointing guns at them. Instead, a man in his mid-sixties came out. The guy had a beer and schnitzel physique, with a red bulbous nose and rosacea spread across puffy cheeks. His gray hair stuck up like he had just had an encounter with high voltage.

Instead of introducing himself, the warehouse man shifted his head toward an inner office. Jake held the door and watched the glaring eyes of the old woman as he closed it on her. The office looked like the aftermath of a hurricane, with papers scattered everywhere. If it were not for the desk legs, Jake would have been surprised the desk was made of wood.

Goran Goluža introduced himself in German, shaking each of their hands but lingering a bit too long with Anica. Yeah, this guy had some serious creep factor, Jake thought. Jake and Anica gave fake names.

The Serb sat behind his desk and Jake moved stacks of paper from two chairs so he and Anica could sit also.

"What can I do for you?" Goluža asked.

Jake paused a beat for impact. "We are here because our organization has been infiltrated by the Polizei."

Goluža sat up straighter in his chair. "That is impossible. Who sent you?"

Now Jake had to be careful. He couldn't just throw lower level names out, even though he didn't have names of anyone higher up the food chain. Luckily, he had spent some time driving and coming up with a plan.

"You are an important asset to us," Jake said.

That seemed to assuage the Serb.

Jake continued, "Our man in Strasbourg just had a run-in with some men trying to disrupt our organization."

Goluža nodded. "I heard about that. He lost one of his men."

"I know," Jake said. "And now the wine man in Riquewihr is missing."

"Pierre. This is the first I have heard of that. What happened?"

"We don't know for sure," Jake said. "But there was a lot of blood involved."

"Jake," came a man's voice in his earpiece. "The truck that just left is owned by a man name Fritz Giger out of Zurich."

"Our people in Switzerland are on high alert, Goran," Jake said.

"I see," Goluža said. "Which ones?"

Thinking quickly, Jake said, "All of them. Zurich, Lucerne, Bern, Geneva."

"I would guess that Austria would be equally concerned," Goluža concluded.

Jake and Anica shared a glance. She got up quickly, pulled out her Glock, and pointed it at the Serb. Then, in Serbian, she said, "Bogdan Maravich was a Polizei informant. He deserved to die."

"That was you?" Goluža asked.

"Put your hands up on the desk," Jake demanded in German, his gun now out also.

Goluža complied, slowly setting his stubby fingers on papers in front of him. "You are the shadow," he said with great deference.

"Jake, we have a problem," came Sirena's voice in Jake's ear.

13

"What do you have?" Jake asked, which brought a strange look from Goran Goluža behind his desk.

"Two cars with at least six men," Sirena said. "Maybe eight."

Jake grasped Anica's arm and whispered, "Time to leave." Then he pointed his gun at Goluža and said, "You just made a huge error. The organization will not be happy with this."

"You mean the Polizei?" Goluža asked, a smirk across his ruddy face.

"I'm not Polizei, asshole," Jake said. He moved around the edge of the man's desk and seriously considered seeing what his new extreme defense ammo would do to a man's skull. Instead, Jake shifted his Glock to his left hand and nearly simultaneously punched the Serb in the mouth, spinning the man around in his chair, his bulbous head eventually slumping to his morbidly obese trunk.

"Why did you do that, Jake?" Anica asked, switching to English. "We needed information from him."

Jake ignored her as he headed toward the door. "Heading out," he said to his comm and those outside.

"They're heading toward the door," Sirena warned.

They got to the outer office and Jake saw that the old woman was gone. She must have gone into the warehouse.

"This way," Jake said.

By the time he opened the door to the warehouse, Jake saw the first man coming through the outer office door. Jake shoved Anica through the warehouse door as he aimed at the armed man. The first man shot at Jake without really aiming, his bullets hitting the wall to his left. But Jake aimed and fired twice. His first bullet struck the man in the throat, and the second round hit the guy just above his left eyebrow.

Jake rushed into the warehouse now and saw a few workers scurrying away. One bay door was open, so that could be their way out. But then a couple of men appeared and started firing at Anica, who returned fire.

The two of them hurried behind a high stack of boxes on pallets.

Now gunfire could be heard outside.

Jake made sure that Anica had good cover as they exchanged fire with these men.

"Are you on them?" Jake asked Sirena or Johann or Rolf.

"We've got them cornered out front," Sirena said. "Two down."

"I also got one coming through the front," Jake said.

The men at the loading dock peppered their position with a massive salvo of bullets striking the boxes in front of Jake and Anica.

"How you doing on ammo?" Jake asked Anica.

"Almost out of the first mag," she said. "But I have two more spares."

"About the same here," Jake said. "Let me hold them off while you back off and come around behind them. There must be another way out."

Anica looked either disturbed or pissed off. "Are you trying to protect me?"

"Always," Jake said. "But it's a sound tactical decision."

She nodded agreement and started to head deeper into the warehouse. As she did so, Jake started a slow and steady stream of gunfire, which kept them pinned down below the loading dock. Then the slide on his Glock slid back, indicating he was out. He quickly dropped the old mag and slapped a full one with 17 rounds into the handle and released the slide, jamming a fresh round into the chamber.

Now he waited for them to make the next move.

"What's happening?" Jake asked everyone on the comm.

More gunfire from outside.

"Polizei are on their way," Sirena said.

Suddenly, the office door opened and Goran Goluža came stumbling out with a gun in his hand. He was followed closely by two other men.

Now Jake had two sets of targets. They had him pinned down.

•

Anica found her way through the tall stacks of pallets toward the back of the warehouse. Here it was much darker than the front area. Occasionally, she would see a worker hunkered down, hiding as best they could behind the pallets.

She walked with stealth as she made her way through the shadowy extremes of the warehouse. Anica could hear various voices speaking German, and guessed these were the workers as well. Then she saw a door ahead. Looking up to the ceiling, she knew this could not be a door to the outside. It had to be another inner office.

Stepping softly ahead, Anica thought about the older woman. Is this where she went?

She saw the gun barrel and instinctively dove to her right just as the shotgun blasted, sending buckshot into a tall pallet behind her. She rolled and aimed at the shooter. Then she fired three shots, dropping the shooter to the concrete floor.

Anica got up and went to the shooter, kicking the shotgun away from the shriveled hands of the old woman. She focused again on the door to nowhere.

Now, as she got closer, she could see that the door had a normal lever handle, but it also had two slide bars reinforcing it. These were not to keep people out of the room. They were to keep something locked inside.

Through her comm earbud Anica could hear speaking in German and English. She could also hear sirens coming. Her friends with German Polizei were on their way. But there was still a lot of gunfire at the front of the warehouse.

But her focus was on this room. She slid the lower bar and hesitated. What could be inside? Anica shoved the upper bar open, and then stopped to consider the handle. As she guessed, she was able to unlock it from her side. Goran Goluža and the old woman were keeping something inside.

Anica opened the door, her gun pointing inside. Then she noticed a light switch at the edge of the door frame. She flipped the lever and strong overhead lights came on revealing the contents of the room.

Huddled against the far wall on the floor were at least a dozen people, mostly younger men. But there were also a couple of women. One even had an infant.

She stayed in the doorframe and said in German, "I am Polizei. You are safe."

Nothing. Maybe they didn't speak German. She repeated the same phrase in English. Still nothing. Then she tried French, and several them seemed to understand this. They could have been North African, she thought. Perhaps Tunisian or Algerian.

In German now, Anica said into her comm what she had found in a back room of the warehouse.

This was confirmation of what she sought as part of her infiltration of this organization. The Serbs and others had built an elaborate underground pipeline, smuggling humans through Europe. This was big business, she thought. And, obviously, business was good.

Jake told her to stay with these people.

•

Now Jake had a good idea what Goran Goluža and his organization was doing. At least partially. Trucking was a good place to hide humans as well as contraband. He guessed if the Polizei went through this warehouse carefully, they would find more than just illegal migrants.

Despite the Polizei arriving out front, they had taken a standoff position—probably until they could get a tactical unit involved. But that didn't help Jake at this time. He was still in an intense firefight, and the only winner might be the one with the most bullets.

Without warning, the chubby old Serb came out from behind his hiding spot firing his weapon like a crazy man. At the same time, the other two men provided cover for Goran Goluža by sending a ton of lead into the boxes in front of Jake.

Aiming carefully, not wanting to kill the old man, Jake fired once at the approaching Serb, hitting the man in the right lower leg. Goran Goluža crumpled to the concrete, his melon hitting the cold surface and knocking him out instantly. With the boss down, the other men started yelling in Serbian.

Into his comm, Jake said, "Goran Goluža has been shot and wounded."

"The Polizei are ready to negotiate," Sirena said. "At first, they wanted to shoot us, but Rolf and Johann flashed their badges. It was intense for a moment. What's your status?"

"I have two douche bags inside here yelling some shit in Serbian," Jake said. "I only understand the swear words."

"Coming your way," Anica said in Jake's ear.

Moments later, Anica came alongside Jake again.

"What are they saying?" she asked him.

"I don't know. I shot Goran Goluža in the leg. Maybe something about that."

"Goluža looks dead," she said.

"He hit his head when he dropped. What did you find back there?"

"Migrants. About a dozen. Mostly young men."

"What about the old woman?"

Anica shook her head.

"Sounded like a shotgun going off," Jake said.

"It was. She almost blew my head off."

Moments later the SWAT team showed up. With Goran Goluža wounded, none of the Serbs wanted to fall on their swords and die for no good reason. The German Polizei would haul everyone in and sort out the good from the bad and the bad from the really bad. Jake had a feeling those working in the warehouse were complicit if not directly involved. There was no way they could not have known about the people hiding in the back room.

It took hours for the local Polizei to unravel what had gone down at this warehouse. Luckily, Rolf and Johann had some pull with the Europol organization, which allowed them to scan through the records Goran Goluža kept in his office. Jake wasn't sure if the Serb would be as anal about recordkeeping as the normal German, but it was likely they would find something.

With Rolf and Johann taking the lead, Jake and Sirena and Anica had been able to stay out of the deep weeds.

When the Polizei ran Jake's Austrian passport, which was real but with the name of his old persona, it was flagged and the Germans were told to let him go. This was still a remnant of what he had done for a former president of Austria, the titular Austrian royal family, and the Grand Master of the Teutonic Knights, headquartered in Vienna. Jake was convinced that Sirena was absolved because she was hot. But in reality, she still had a lot of pull in the CIA and with the Israeli government.

Jake and Sirena sat in their rental BMW waiting to hear back from Johann and Rolf, who were still in the warehouse reviewing documents.

"What do you think?" Sirena asked from the passenger seat.

"I think we need to do something with the Frenchman in the trunk of our car," Jake said.

She laughed. "I forgot all about him. We might also need to part ways with the boys from Austria."

Jake watched as Anica discussed her part in the take-down of this operation with a high-ranking German Polizei officer across the parking lot.

"She handled herself quite well," Sirena said. "She's a good officer."

"She is. But I think any cover she had has been blown."

"I agree."

"It doesn't mean she needs to go back to Innsbruck," Jake reasoned.

Sirena looked at Jake critically. "You were tasked to find her. You did that."

"I know," Jake said. "But they've already found a ton of drugs in this warehouse. Maybe we should cross over into Switzerland and see where this case leads. We could check on this Fritz Giger fellow."

"That makes sense. When I talked with the people smuggled into Germany, they said they were transported from Switzerland in Giger's truck."

"Good thing you speak Arabic," Jake said.

"Anica did alright with her French."

"Here she comes. Let's see what she says."

Jake lowered the driver's window and Anica leaned in to talk. "They want me to write up a report on what happened."

"The Germans like their reports," Jake said. "What about Rolf and Johann?"

"They're still going through the files," Anica said. "But I'll need to stay here and help them, since some of the documents are in Serbian."

Jake checked his watch. "Sounds like you might be a while."

"Perhaps," Anica said. "But then I will head to Zurich. Thank you for your help. Both of you. I couldn't have done this without you."

"This is a big win, Anica," Jake said. "How is your boss in Innsbruck dealing with this?"

"Sabine Bauer? I talked with her briefly and explained the situation. Rolf has agreed to take Pierre Deval to The Hague for interrogation."

"I didn't realize that Europol was doing stuff like that," Jake said.

"Not normally," Anica said. "But with our investigation now in France, Germany and Austria, it makes sense. Rolf will make sure to at least get copies of all documents found in the warehouse."

"All right," Jake said. "We can stick with you."

Anica shook her head. "That's not necessary, Uncle Jake."

"It wasn't necessary for me to come here to look for you," he said. "But some things you do because you must do so."

She glanced at the warehouse and then back to Jake and said, "Those people are just looking for a better life, much like I was as a young girl."

"It's not the same," he said. "You had just lost both of your parents and had no way to make a living. You were a young girl. Most of these people are working-aged men. I understand their despair and their plight. But there are legal ways to emigrate to European countries. This is not the way. People are exploiting them. You saw how they were locked in that room like animals. That's not the right way to handle this crisis."

"Then we must stop them," Anica said defiantly.

Jake put his hand on Anica's forearm. "You are a good person, Anica. You have a great heart." He checked his watch again. "I don't think the Serb had time to warn anyone of this raid. And we wrapped up all the players. Make sure the German Polizei doesn't allow them to call anyone."

"I have already told them," Anica said. "I told them we still have the big fish to catch. That should give us a couple of days."

"Sounds like you might be here for the night," Jake said. "I think we'll head over to Zurich and get eyes on Fritz Giger."

"That would be very helpful, since we are not a hundred percent sure that Goran Goluža didn't call someone while we were occupied with the shooters."

"Well, I did knock him out," Jake said. "But he still might have had time to call someone. It is what it is now. We'll just have to work with it." He pulled the keys and got out, rounding the BMW to the trunk. "Are you sure you don't want me to drop off this French asshole out in the country somewhere?"

Anica shrugged. "We should probably do this by the book."

A little too late for that, Jake thought. Then he gave Anica a big hug and whispered into her ear, "I'll see you in Zurich."

She kissed Jake on the cheek. "Take care."

With nobody looking, Jake popped the trunk and dragged Pierre out. The Frenchman was a little wobbly on his feet. The pillowcase over his head was caked with dried blood and probably drool.

Jake said to Pierre, "Listen you fucking dirtbag. If you mention how you got the bruises on your face, I'll come back and cut off your balls. You understand?"

"Yes, ja, oui," Pierre said.

Smiling, Jake roughly handed the man over to Anica, who took him to one of the German Polizei cars.

Then Jake got back into the rental BMW and put the key in the ignition.

"Everything alright?" Sirena asked.

"Roger that. We stay in Zurich tonight."

"How long is that drive?"

"About an hour."

Sirena sat back against the leather seats. "Sounds like nap time."

14

Zurich, Switzerland

Jake and Sirena checked into the Schwangau Hotel in downtown Zurich. It was a five-star six-hundred-year-old hotel that hugged the Limmat River, which drained from Zurichsee, the massive lake to the east of the city. Jake had once stayed at a villa on the south shore of the lake with Alexandra. He was quite familiar with this city, which is why he decided to pay so much for a hotel stay. The Schwangau was an elegant display of Swiss architecture, but it was also just across the Weinplatz from the import/export offices of Fritz Giger's company.

Sitting at a small table in his room, Jake browsed a pamphlet from the hotel. "Interesting fact," Jake said. "Finally, this place makes sense. Zurich was a tax collection point in the Roman Empire. Back then it was called Turicum."

Sirena, who had recently gotten out of the shower and put on what little make-up she used, came over to Jake and put her hands on her hips. "It's more ironic, right?"

"Because it's a tax haven now?"

"Right. And one of the largest banking cities in the world."

Jake got up and gave her a big hug. Then he pulled back slightly and kissed her on the lips.

"What was that for?" she asked.

"Just because. We haven't had a lot of time to talk since we left The Azores. We have some time now while we wait for our sources to provide intel."

She hugged him and kissed him before sitting down on the bed. "This isn't our fight."

He paced in front of her. Jake had a feeling she was thinking this way. It made sense. More sense than putting each of them in danger. "I know," Jake finally said.

"She's a capable young woman. She reminds me of a younger me."

He smiled. "I was thinking that as well." Jake pulled out a chair from the small table and sat on it backwards, his arms holding onto the back. Then he continued, "When I first heard she was missing, I wasn't sure what to think. I didn't know if I could handle another person in my life meeting a tragic end."

"I understand. We've also had some close calls over the years. I worry about you."

Jake studied her carefully. Usually, Sirena was a straight shooter. What you see is what you got. But now she seemed to be coming at their current dilemma from a more obtuse angle. "Obviously, I worry about your safety. Why do you think I wanted us to take assignments unlike that one in Morocco?"

"Or South America."

"Right. I assumed this would not be like any of those operations. It was a simple missing person case."

She swiveled her head side to side. "Jake, you could turn an Easter egg hunt into a Mafia bloodbath."

He raised his hands palm out in protest. "Hey, it might seem that way in the aggregate of events. But bad shit happens to me about four or five times a year. That's a small percentage of my normal life."

"I hear you. But tell me this. Based on your life, would any reasonable insurance company give you a policy?"

"It's a specious argument," Jake said. "I have enough money stashed away. I don't need life insurance."

"That's not the point, of course."

He knew exactly what she was getting at. Which is why he had stashed his infant daughter in Montana with his two siblings. "That's why I'm an unfit father to Emma."

"No, that's what makes you a good father. You put her there to protect her."

"It's why Toni never told me about my son Karl," Jake said.

She stood up and seemed angry. "I don't want to fight."

He rose from his chair and put his hands on her shoulders. "This isn't a fight. This is a logical discussion. You think I'm blinded by my love for Anica. That I might go too far to protect her."

"I don't think you ever go too far, Jake. You always do what's necessary. That's why I love you."

He pulled her close to his body. This was the first time she had said the L word. "I love you, too," he said into her ear.

They held each other now for a long moment, until Jake's phone suddenly buzzed in his pocket. He pulled out his SAT phone and saw that it was from a friend and former colleague in the old Swiss intelligence service, which had about a decade ago morphed into the Federal Intelligence Service. The FIS was like the FBI and CIA of Switzerland.

"Yeah," Jake said. "What do you have on our friend?" When Jake found out he was coming to Switzerland, he had asked for help doing a background of Fritz Giger.

"Let's meet in the platz below," the FIS officer said. "Ten minutes."

Jake hung up and shoved his phone into his pocket again.

"Your FIS friend?" she asked.

"Yeah."

"He doesn't want to talk on the phone."

"Right. I told him my phone was extremely secure and encrypted, so he must be worried about his end."

Sirena sat back on the bed. "You want to do this alone?"

"I think it would be better. Hans Disler is easily distracted by pretty women. He's never been married and has always been quite the player."

She smiled and said, "Are you sure you won't be a distraction to him?"

"Funny. Could you check with the Spaniard's people and see what they know about Fritz Giger and his company?"

"They said they'd get back with me."

"They need to work on our time, not their time."

"I'll poke at them."

Jake checked his gun and then slung on his leather jacket before leaving her alone in their room.

Weinplatz was not a huge public square. At night, it was lit by street lamps with multiple globes that ran alongside the pedestrian bridge over the river. There were only a few businesses here, and fewer open. So, Jake should would have no problem finding his old friend and colleague.

Hans was an unassuming man in his late fifties. He was a chunky, short man that nobody would mistake for a prototypical spy. That's what made him so good, Jake thought.

Instead of standing in one place, Jake wandered slowly through the platz, turning occasionally to watch his six. The river seemed to be running stronger than normal. Considering the cold, damp evening, the area was in heavy use this evening—mostly younger couples and pensioners strolling slowly after a large dinner.

Jake got to the bridge and finally saw his contact approaching from the shadows near the Rathaus. Hans had his waddle on, and his normally ubiquitous cigarette had been replaced with a vape stick.

Hans came up to Jake like the old friend he was and shook hands. "Nice to see an old friend," Hans said.

Smiling, Jake said, "You're older."

"Not by much, I would guess." Hans sucked on his vape stick and let out a stream of steam.

"Gave up on cigarettes for something a little healthier," Jake said.

"Doctor's orders. Now, instead of being addicted to tobacco, I'm addicted to this damn e-cigarette. Nicotine is the guilty culprit in this whole thing. Do you think the makers of these could do so without an addicting agent?"

"I'm sure they could," Jake agreed. "But this way they don't kill you as fast and can keep you as a customer longer. At least until you die by natural causes."

Hans raised his bushy brows and smiled behind his vape stick. "You're a cynical bastard."

"Some things never change, my friend. What do you have for me?"

"No foreplay," Hans said. "Just stick it in and ram it home."

"I'm not working on the government's dime anymore," Jake said.

"I'm done in two months."

"Are they putting you out to pasture?"

"Quite literally," the Swiss man said. "I've considered buying a country home overlooking a lake. I might keep a few sheep and cattle. Maybe some chickens to give me eggs."

"Sounds nice. Are you sure you don't want me to put a bullet in your head now?"

Hans laughed. "When that time comes, you will be my first call."

Jake waited now for the soon to be former spy to divulge what he knew about Fritz Giger.

Finally, Hans said, "This Giger fellow has been under investigation by our agency and the Swiss Federal Polizei for a number of years for a number of problems."

"So, he's not just exporting coocoo clocks and cheese."

"No. But we have not been able to make anything stick with him."

"Follow the money. Maybe he's being protected by the Polizei."

"How did Fritz Giger come across your radar?" Hans asked.

Jake explained the bust that just went down in Germany, and how they had tracked the truck to Giger's company.

"So, German Polizei knows about this?" Hans asked.

"Not yet. We left out some of that to give us time. If the Germans decide to coordinate with your government, Giger's operation could be alerted. I'm guessing a guy like that would have a contingency plan to close up shop."

"What makes you think he hasn't found out about what happened in Konstanz?"

"I didn't mention Konstanz," Jake said. "How did you find out?"

Hans delayed by shoving his vape stick in his mouth and puffing on it like a high school kid attacking a joint for the first time. His eyes shifted around and

Jake realized this guy would make a terrible poker player. Finally, Hans said, "I can't say."

He just did, Jake reasoned. They had someone in Giger's company undercover. "Then Fritz Giger knows about what happened in Konstanz."

Hans shook his head. "We don't think so."

"Then your man was undercover in Konstanz," Jake concluded. "Did this man shoot at me?"

"Of course not," Hans said, and then must have realized he had given away more than he intended. "You do this to me every time. You're a bastard."

"I've been told this." Then Jake glanced about the small square and turned back to his old friend. "The man and woman on the far end are with you. They're pretending to be a couple, but clearly the man is gay and is repulsed by the woman. Behind me on the bridge is an older man sitting alone, but struggling not to look this way. Am I that dangerous that you need this kind of backup?"

"Do you need to even ask that question?"

"But we're friends, Hans."

"That's what I told my boss. But he insisted I bring a few friends."

Jake could understand that sentiment. "How many people do you have watching Giger?"

Hans shrugged. "Maybe a couple."

Now Jake had an idea which way to go. The Swiss had their hands tied. "You mentioned that Giger might be protected by your Polizei."

"I didn't implicate the Polizei," Hans corrected. "It could be a prominent politician or businessman. Perhaps a banker."

"I'm not constrained like you and the FIS," Jake said.

"True."

Jake smiled, knowing that his old friend had banked on this fact. "So, you let me talk with the man and I'll make sure to give you everything I find out."

Hans made a struggled attempt to delay, sucking in more vapor. Then he said, "That sounds fair. As long as you promise not to kill him."

"Giger has to think I will."

"I understand."

"Deal. Now, you need to tell me everything you currently have on the man, even if it is only speculation and can't be proven at this time."

Hans agreed. Then he went through everything the FIS had discovered so far. Jake was sure the Swiss man was telling him the truth. He knew not to lie to Jake.

"All right," Jake said. "You don't have a last name on this Jakov fellow?"

"Afraid not. We don't have a location for the man, either. But we think he might be the man at the top."

Drugs, human trafficking, bribery of politicians, etc. This criminal organization was making a big move across Europe.

"We can't be involved with anything you do," Hans said.

"That's fine with me. All I ask is you and your people stay the hell out of my way."

"You have my word," Hans said. Then he pulled out his phone and typed in something.

A few seconds later Jake's phone buzzed in his pocket.

"That's Giger's address," Hans said. "He's there right now."

Jake didn't bother checking his phone. He trusted Hans to play it straight. He wandered back the platz toward his hotel, knowing this could be the last time he saw his old Swiss friend. The guy looked beaten down, Jake thought. Hans Disler deserved to retire.

15

Innsbruck, Austria

Sabine Bauer sat in the back corner of the bar in the old town of the city. As the Kriminal Hauptkommisar of Tirol, she would normally require a security detail, especially with the increase in crime recently. However, she had ordered her normal Polizei detail to take the night off.

She wanted this meeting to be off the record, which is why she was dressed a bit more provocatively than normal, with designer jeans, leather boots to just below her knees, and a tight silk top that did nothing to hide her substantial breasts. If you've got them, flaunt them, she thought. Especially when they could help her get certain information from a man. She sipped on a whiskey sour and set it back on the wooden table in front of her.

Her contact walked into the bar now, stopped to get a beer, and then wandered over to her table. He was a handsome man, she thought. Strong and beefy from top to bottom, unlike so many other men in Europe of late. But he also had a certain arrogance lingering about his aura.

Verner Kappel was a German national, and a former high-ranking official of their Polizei. Now he served as Deputy Director of Operations at Europol in The Hague.

Sitting across from Sabine, Verner said, "I'm glad we could meet." He reached his hand across the table and the two of them shook warmly.

"I always have time for you, Verner," she said. Although the man was in his early 50s, he was still very desirable. He was like Jake Adams without the possibility of the man putting a bullet in her head.

"As you know, we have a couple of your officers in the field working on an important case," Verner said.

"Of course."

"And you know of the European Migrant Smuggling Centre."

"Yes. EMSC is becoming more and more prominent in the EU."

"We believe that Anica has made a significant bust today in Germany."

Sabine checked her watch. It was nearly past midnight. "Almost yesterday."

"Right. But she did not do this alone. What can you tell me about her friends?" Verner took a long drink of his beer as he studied her reaction.

"You mean Rolf and Johann," she said, routinely. "You know Rolf Fischer. Johann is our most recent liaison with Europol."

"Why was Johann Gruber involved?"

Interesting. He already knew the man's surname. "As far as I can tell, it was personal with Johann. He was working with Anica when she was nearly killed here recently. Then Anica went missing. I authorized him to find Anica. She might be currently working with Europol, but she is still a Tirol Polizei asset."

"I understand," Verner said. "But is she reporting to you or to us?"

That was the best question the man could ask, but not one in which she would answer truthfully. "I have not heard from Anica since before she went missing in the river that night." Actually, that was the truth.

Verner bore his eyes through her as he twisted his glass of beer in a circle on the table. "What about the former intelligence officers working with Anica?"

She tried not to respond nonverbally, but she hesitated too long. "I know nothing about anyone other than Rolf and Johann."

The German from Europol let out a little chuckle under his breath. "So, you don't know Jake Adams?"

Now she had no choice but to acknowledge this man. "Of course. He was a resident of Innsbruck for many years. Why do you ask about him?"

"He is with Anica."

"Herr Adams was like an uncle to her," Sabine said. "But I understand he has been retired for some time."

"Men like Adams never retire," Verner said. "Not until they get a bullet to the head."

"Many have tried to kill Herr Adams," Sabine said. "If he is with Anica, then I feel much better about her safety."

Verner took a long drink of beer, leaving just a tiny amount in the bottom of his glass. "If you happen to hear from Anica or this Adams fellow, you make it clear that he is to stay out of this."

"I have no sway over this man," she said. "He is a private citizen."

He shook his head and got up to leave. Instead of a professional handshake, Verner simply lifted his chin and smirked before leaving.

Sabine waved her thumb at the bartender, meaning to bring her another drink.

Then, she picked up her phone and touched a contact from her office. When the young man picked up with a simple ja, she said, "Do you have him?"

"Yes, ma'am. He got into a taxi out front and we're following him now."

"Good. Stick with him. I need to know where he goes and who he sees."

"*Ja, Kriminal Hauptkommisar.*"

Something wasn't right about that man's visit, she thought. He could have simply picked up the phone and asked her these same questions. But for some reason Verner Kappel wanted to do this in person. Why? Hopefully her officers would find out tonight.

The bartender brought her another drink, and she immediately sipped on the fresh whiskey sour.

How in the hell had Verner found out about Jake Adams? There was no way that Anica had told him. And it wasn't likely that Johann had any contact with Verner. So that left just one man. Rolf. But why mention Adams? She took out her phone and pulled up her contact list. Sabine was about to send Jake a text and let him know that Europol knew he was involved. But then she decided to wait and see why Verner was really in Innsbruck.

She put her phone back in her purse and sipped on her drink.

16

Zurich, Switzerland

Jake and Sirena sat a block down the street from the three-story home owned by Fritz Giger. It wasn't hard to find the Swiss intelligence officers staking out the house along this quiet residential street. There was a car posted on either side of the block, strategically situated for an unobstructed view of Giger's front door and his tuck-under garage. Even though it was just past midnight, several of the houses still had lights on, including Giger's house, which still had illumination on the third floor. The bedroom, Jake guessed.

"What if Giger knows about Konstanz?" Sirena asked.

"I doubt it. If he did, the man would more than likely have some visible security. Let's go."

Sirena took off her seat belt and said, "How do you plan to get in?"

He smiled. "The easiest way possible."

He got out and strolled down the sidewalk, stopping at the FIS car surveilling the house. Tapping on the window of the driver, which nearly made the man behind the wheel jump out of his skin, the younger man finally lowered his window. Jake told him in German that he would take it from here. They were dismissed. Hans must have done his job, since the man didn't complain. If fact, they called the other car at the end of the street and both cars slowly pulled away.

Then Jake and Sirena walked up to the front door and stood for a moment. "No security," Jake said. Then he rang the doorbell and waited.

"You think he's just going to open the door for you?" Sirena asked.

"Yep. The Swiss are terminally nice people. Not much crime here."

Sirena glanced up and down the street. "Much more with you here."

As predicted, Fritz Giger came down wearing actual pajamas in a blue and pink Batman pattern. Giger hesitated for a microsecond before opening his thick wooden door.

"What brings the Polizei by my house so late," Giger asked in German.

"May we come in?" Jake asked.

Giger waved his hand and let them through his threshold, closing the door behind them.

"Please take off your shoes," Giger said. "These floors are Brazilian cherry."

Jake thought for a moment, wondering how he wanted to play this meeting. He could go harsh or play it straight. Giger already thought he was Polizei, so he thought it might be best to play up that angle for now. So, they took off their shoes. Then he noticed that Giger was wearing pink bunny slippers.

They knew that Giger was not married, had never been so, and had no children. Jake's gaydar had often been wrong in the past, but he was pretty damn sure that Fritz Giger was coming up as a logical and likely blip on his screen. Jake had considered using Sirena to entice the man, but now he knew he might have to go there himself.

Giger led them into a lower level study. Instead of wood and masculine fixtures, this area looked like Liberace had spewed his man juices all over the place. The furniture was red velvet. Frilly lamps looked to be straight out of an 1800s bordello. There was no desk in the room, only those plush chairs around a heart-shaped table of glass trimmed in gold leaf. Yeah, the man was flaming, Jake thought.

"May I get you officers a drink?" Giger asked.

"Sorry, sir, but we are on duty," Jake declared.

"You don't mind if I drink," the Swiss man said.

"Go for it."

The man poured himself a brown liquid from a crystal decanter and then took a seat and crossed his legs like a woman, exposing legs without any hair whatsoever.

"What can I do for you fine officers?" Giger asked, his gaze undressing Jake and not Sirena.

Jake took a seat closer to the Swiss man, while Sirena sat across from them.

"We have a problem," Jake said.

Giger pouted his lips. "I don't like problems."

"Neither does the organization."

"The Polizei?"

"The other organization," Jake said.

Giger shook his shoulders. "I don't understand."

Jake knew that wasn't true. Hans had given him enough information to hang the man, and Sirena had gotten more info from their people. So, Jake was certain he could make his ruse work.

"The supply chain could be compromised," Jake finally said.

"You will have to be more specific," Giger said. "I have more than a hundred trucks through every European country, with the exception of Belarus. I still don't trust those people."

"Jakov," Jake said.

With the sound of that name, Giger's eyes got large. The Swiss man couldn't hold back his nervousness now. He quickly drank his drink and got up to pour himself more. "Are you sure you don't want some?"

Jake waved the man off.

This time Giger had nearly filled his crystal glass to the top with the alcohol. He sat down delicately and sipped his drink.

"Jakov," Jake repeated.

"What does he want now?" Giger asked. "Have I not given him enough?"

The Swiss man would find out sooner or later, Jake thought. So, he decided to use some real information to get some unknown information.

"Goran Goluža was arrested earlier today, along with confiscation of our most recent shipment."

Giger sucked down a third of his drink. "Those from North Africa?"

"Yes. Along with the drugs he stored there. We think the Frenchman sold him out."

"Pierre? Too bad. I like his tiny little penis. He is like a ten-year-old child. Doesn't rip you a new colon every time. Why do you suspect Pierre told the Polizei about Goran?"

Jake glanced at Sirena, who looked about as disinterested as humanly possible. Then Jake said, "Pierre is also in German Polizei custody."

Giger waved his hand and scoffed. "Jakov Koprivica must be livid."

Finally, they had the man's surname. "You could say that," Jake said. "Jakov is not a pleasant man to begin with, so you can imagine now. I will be meeting with him tomorrow. Is there anything you could tell him to calm him down?"

"Jakov is in Switzerland?" Giger asked.

"I didn't say that."

"Yes, of course. I know he hates Zurich."

"As you know, we have operations all over the country, from Lucerne to Interlaken." He was fishing, but pretty sure about both locations, based on information from Hans.

"Jakov does love Interlaken," Giger said. "It must have something to do with ski towns. Although I can't imagine that rotund man on skis."

"Is that what you want me to tell him tomorrow?" Jake asked.

"Now, you are just playing with me," Giger said. And under his breath he added, "I wish."

Jake waited for the Swiss man to say something, but he must have forgotten the question. "What can you tell me that will satisfy Jakov tomorrow?"

Giger finished his drink, his eyes flitting about the room. "Does she never talk?"

"Her German is not great," Jake said. "And she's the strong silent type."

Raising his brows, Giger said, "Likes it on top?"

"Easy. If she knew what you just said, she would slit your throat."

Sirena was ignoring the men as she clicked away on her phone.

Now Giger looked concerned and turned to Sirena. "I'm sorry," he said. Then he twisted back toward Jake. "What language does she speak?"

"Kurdish. But that's not important. Answer my damn question. Jakov will be concerned about your routes through Italy once the Polizei discovers that's how the people in German custody entered the European Union."

"You are Polizei. You can handle this."

"We have no control over INTERPOL and others," Jake said.

"The Italians will never be a problem," Giger said. "With the Mafia and the corrupt Polizia, our pipeline will never get clogged there. They don't want the people to stay. As soon as they hit the shores, they shove them into buses and send them north."

Jake already knew this. But he wasn't sure how the Italians got away with dumping them across the borders into France, Switzerland, Austria or Slovenia. Yet, he couldn't ask this question directly or he would give away the fact that he didn't work for the organization.

"The Germans are starting to crack down on these people," Jake said. "So is Austria."

"Jakov has Austria covered," Giger said, taking Jake's bait.

"Maybe so. But if INTERPOL or the EU decides to take a strong stand against more people entering the member countries, we could be in trouble."

"Is that not why we use Switzerland for staging?" Giger asked. "We are not part of the EU. But we still maintain strong trade with the member countries."

Jake gave the man a stern gaze.

Giger, sensing Jake was not going away without some reassurance, said, "Tell Jakov I will complete a top to bottom review of our operation. Also, ask him if I will be dealing with you from now on, or Giovanni again."

Jake thought quickly. "Which Giovanni? We have three in our organization, not including lower level people."

"Giovanni Caspari from Lake Como," Giger said. "I know what you mean, though. The Italians should consider a few more given names."

Thinking he might have overplayed his hand, Jake got up and shook the Swiss man's limp paw.

Giger led them to the front door and then furled his brows and said, "You didn't mention your name."

By now, Sirena was out onto the front porch, but still playing with her phone like a distracted teenager.

Jake gave Giger a disturbed look. "You're right. Most simply call me the fixer. It's better if you don't know. You understand."

"Of course," Giger said, but he didn't understand.

Leaving the man in the Batman pajamas slack jawed and confused, Jake met Sirena out on the sidewalk and the two of them wandered in the darkness toward their rental BMW.

Sirena nuzzled next to Jake and said, "I do like it on top."

"Either way works for me."

"You were brilliant in there," she said.

"Hope you got the two names."

"What do you think I was doing, checking my social media status?"

Since Jake knew she didn't have any social media presence, he simply said, "Get anything?"

"Our people are looking into both men."

He put his arm around her and brought his head to hers, whispering, "Did you notice the cars?"

"Of course. Both Fords. One behind us and the other about a block behind our car. People in both. They ducked down a little too late."

"Those aren't the FIS cars," Jake said.

"Right. Those were Audis."

They got to the BMW and Jake made sure to ignore the Ford sitting a block behind them. He clicked the doors open and got behind the wheel. She buckled herself into the passenger seat.

"Ready to take a ride?" he asked her.

"Why not," she said. "You haven't scared the shit out of me in a while."

Jake turned over the engine and pulled out slowly from the curb.

Sirena turned the large screen on the dash to the GPS map.

"Good idea," Jake said. "I've plotted out a route in my mind, but they might force us to go elsewhere."

Glancing in the rearview mirror, Jake saw the Ford pull out and follow him. Then, as they approached the second Ford, he saw the driver's window come down and what had to be a gun barrel.

He punched it, lurching the BMW forward immediately. Those in the Ford had no time to react.

They shot at their BMW, but none of the bullets struck their car.

Jake turned right at the first corner, the BMW hugging the corner like a Formula One car.

"This heads toward downtown," Sirena warned.

"I know."

At that time of night, or early morning, the roads were nearly absent of cars. So, Jake was able to easily power around the slower cars.

Jake occasionally glanced at the large GPS screen on the dash, but he mostly relied on his knowledge of the city and instinct to navigate the narrow streets, making sure not to turn down dead ends.

"Who are these people?" Sirena asked as she glanced over her shoulder.

"My guess is they're part of the organization," he said. "Probably coming to meet with Giger to let him know in person about Konstanz. Just like we did."

"But how did they know to follow us? To chase us?"

"I don't know. I'm trying to drive."

"They're moving in on us."

He knew they could keep up with him on the side streets, but the BMW would blow them away on the autobahn. Jake could see signs for the Number 1

Autobahn ahead. He knew this was a ring road around the city, so he ran a red light and then cranked the wheel hard, hitting the gas and sliding through the intersection. He jammed the gas hard once the car straightened out, slapping them back into their leather seats as they flew up the autobahn onramp.

Once they got on the autobahn, Jake looked back and saw that the two Fords had not come up the ramp yet. Did he really want to lose these guys? Or would it be better to confront them? What if they were FIS or Swiss Polizei? No, he needed to escape these people. Especially with what they had found out from Giger.

Finally, Jake saw the Fords enter the autobahn. Checking the speedometer, he saw that they were cruising at 220 kilometers per hour.

When they came upon another car, it was always in the slower lanes, so they simply whipped past them.

Eventually, Autobahn 1 turned into Autobahn 3, and they came around the south side of the city. Now Jake had a choice to make. He could turn south on Autobahn 4, or continue on 3 along the south side of Lake Zurich. He could also come around and reenter the city from the south and head back toward their hotel. Looking back, he couldn't see the Fords anywhere because of the curve in the road. He slipped past

Autobahn 4, but those behind him might guess that he had turned onto that road. Ahead, he slowed just enough to navigate the split of Autobahn 3. Instead of following the autobahn south along the lake, Jake turned left and started to slow somewhat.

"Do you see anything back there?" Jake asked.

Sirena turned and tried to see if the Fords where anywhere in view. "You lost them."

To be sure, Jake got off the autobahn at the first exit and headed onto side streets toward downtown Zurich.

Now they were traveling at the posted speed limit, not wanting to pick up any Polizei. Jake was surprised they had not been tracked by them.

"Giger's house was bugged," Jake concluded.

"You think so? By who?"

"I don't know. But I hope it was the FIS, otherwise the organization knows we have the names of two higher-level operatives."

"Now what?" she asked.

"Now we go back to the hotel and get our money's worth."

"Sounds good. I get horny with danger," she said.

That wasn't what he was thinking, but he said, "Sounds like a plan."

17

Anica Senka drove slowly down the quiet Zurich neighborhood. She was tired from the drive from Konstanz, Germany, even though it was not that far away. The problem was the hour—it was nearly two in the morning.

Sitting in the passenger side was Johann Gruber, her former Austrian Polizei partner. Rolf Fisher had split off from them in Germany, taking the lead in interrogating both Pierre Deval and Goran Goluža. Based on her knowledge of Serbian, Anica thought she should have been the one to interrogate that man. But by the time they left Konstanz, the man was just getting out of surgery for his leg wound. Jake's bullet had hit a bone and shattered it, which meant Goluža needed some major work done. He would be in recovery mode for a few days.

She pulled over to the curb about a block down the street from her target location—the house of Fritz Giger.

"Have you heard back from Jake?" Johann asked.

Anica shook her head. "Not yet. But it's late. He's probably sleeping."

Johann laughed. "He is old. Needs his sleep."

"I'll tell him you said so."

"No. Don't."

"What's the matter?"

Shaking his head, Johann said, "That man is scary."

Jake was that, she thought. Unless he was on your side. But Johann needed to have a healthy respect for the man. "I wouldn't mess with him. Let's go."

"Are you sure we should talk to the man at this hour?" Johann asked.

"We have to move forward," she said. "What if somehow the organization found out about the raid in Konstanz?"

"I thought that's why Jake came here."

He had a point. "But I haven't heard from him."

Johann checked his watch. "We could wait until morning now. At least four hours. A reasonable hour."

She pulled the keys and got out. Before closing the door, she leaned back in and said, "Maybe you'd like to stay back here and do your nails. But I'm going in."

Johann mumbled something.

"What?"

"I said you seem to be turning into the female version of Jake. He's rubbing off on you." But Johann unbuckled and got out.

The two of them walked casually, like a young couple coming in from a night on the town, down the sidewalk toward Giger's house.

At the man's front door, Anica hesitated long enough to pull out her Europol credentials. Johann did the same thing.

She rang the doorbell and waited.

Nothing.

"Maybe he's not home," Johann said.

"Did you hear that?"

"What?"

"I heard someone moving around in there," she said.

"He probably doesn't want to answer the door at this hour. It's understandable."

She checked the door lever. It was unlocked. Now she drew her Glock and stepped through the front door. She heard a slight noise, like a door closing softly.

With her gun aimed in front of her, a small flashlight in her left hand, Anica swept through the first floor of the house. The place was trashed, especially a library area.

They used hand signals to move through the man's house. Nothing on the first floor.

Johann took the lead up the staircase. Once they reached the top, he went to the right into what must have been a spare bedroom, while she held her position.

Then she took the lead down the hallway, poking into a bathroom and finding nothing.

They were aided by a series of night lights illuminating the hallway. The final door at the end of the hall was partially open.

Anica leaned into the door and it slowly opened on the room. Her flashlight caught something on the floor, so she moved in quickly until she could see the full scene. Laying on the floor on his back, in blue and pink Batman pajamas, was Fritz Giger. His chest had two spots of blood that seemed to be still oozing and pooling along each side of his trunk. One more blood spot sat between his eyes, and a remarkably small circle of blood seeped from behind his head.

"*Scheisse*," Anica mumbled. Had Jake done this to the man? She took out her phone and shot several photos. The best angle she sent quickly to Jake.

Johann also had his phone out, but he was calling this in to the local Polizei.

"Did you hear that?" she asked, shoving her phone back in her pocket and aiming her gun toward the hallway. "Someone's coming."

By now Johann had the Polizei on the phone and he was giving them their location.

She saw lights coming up the staircase down the hall, so she yelled, "Polizei."

Those down the hallway yelled back that they were with FIS, Swiss Federal Intelligence Service. The next few minutes were chaotic, as a number of men rushed in and they all aimed guns at each other.

Eventually, someone had to give way, so Johann put his gun back in its holster while he slowly pulled out his Europol credentials and handed it to the man who seemed to be in charge, an older guy who looked like he survived on a diet of beer and bratwurst. This man then showed Johann his identification, who let Anica take a look as well.

Anica was satisfied, putting her gun away. Then she took out her own ID and let the Swiss man look it over.

The Swiss man handed back Anica's ID and studied the scene quickly. "Did you two kill this man?"

"No," Johann protested. "He was dead when we got here."

"What were you looking for?" the Swiss man asked.

"We didn't trash the place," Anica said. "But we think we might have just missed the killer."

"Why are you here?"

"May I call you Hans?" she asked.

He shrugged. "That's my name." Then he pulled out a vape stick and pulled in a long stream of vapor.

Anica quickly mentioned that she had made a bust in Konstanz and tracked that to Fritz Giger here in Zurich. She was simply coming here to talk with the man.

"Strange hour to talk with a suspect," Otto said.

"I could say the same of you and your men," she said. Suddenly, her phone buzzed and she took it out, seeing that it was Jake. He simply said to call him.

"A man is dead and you play with your phone?" Hans asked, as he squinted his eyes through the vapor cloud.

She quickly texted Jake, saying the FIS was there. Her phone rang almost immediately.

"Hello," she said.

"The FIS," Jake said. "A dumpy older man prone to vaping?"

"How?"

"Never mind," Jake said. "Put him on the line."

Anica handed her phone to the Swiss man, who looked a little confused. She could still hear Jake a little on the other end. Uncle Jake was raising his voice, she thought with a smile.

"I see," Hans said. "I understand."

Now the Swiss man's eyes concentrated on Anica, but she couldn't hear what Jake was saying.

"I will," Hans said, nodding his head in agreement. Then he handed the phone back to Anica and said, "I'm sorry. I did not know you were friends with Jake."

Anica smiled and got on with Jake again. "Is everything alright?"

"It is now," Jake said. "Get out of there and come to my hotel." He gave her the name of the place and his room number.

"Are you sure? I have Johann with me."

"I'm not getting back to sleep now," Jake said. "You can share a king-sized bed with Sirena. Johann can take the sofa in the other room."

"Alright, Uncle Jake. We'll be there soon."

"Oh, and watch out for a couple of dark late-model Fords," he said.

"Why?"

"Just be careful," he said. Then he hung up.

Anica turned back to the Swiss man and said, "If I can help in any way, please let me know."

"We've got this," Hans said.

She gave Johann a head and eye roll, and her friend followed her out of the house.

18

Jake's neck was a little sore the next morning. With Anica and Sirena taking the bed, and Johann on the sofa, Jake had eventually settled into a plush chair by a window overlooking Weinplatz. His thought that he could not get back to sleep had been false, but he continued to wake abruptly, his neck flinging up with each start. His mind could not quite let this case go. He knew he should have simply packed his little duffle bag and flown back to The Azores with Sirena and continue his fishing adventures there. Tuna would be in full swing now, and with the increase in Atlantic water temps coming, the marlin would be running strong soon.

He had left the others upstairs in the room to get more sleep, while Jake went downstairs to the square for a cappuccino and apple strudel. Jake had finished his pastry and his first coffee when he got a text with an attached file from an old colleague at the CIA. He punched in his encryption code to access the file and started to read the files on two men—Giovanni Caspari and Jakov Koprivica. The Italian was suspected of having ties with organized crime in northern Italy, which was not as established as the Malavita in Calabria and Sicily. Caspari also had ties to politicians in the Italian Region of Lombardy. But those ties were suspected to extend all the way to Rome. Yeah, Jake thought, the guy had protection. He was more than likely the conduit for the stream of contraband heading north through Switzerland. The text also had contact information on Caspari, from his home in the Lake Como area of Italy, to his business and second home in Lucerne, Switzerland. Neither of those places were cheap areas to live, so Caspari must have had money.

The information on Koprivica was spotty at best. His military career, like so many others from the Balkan states, had holes you could drive a tank through. He had started out as a lieutenant in the Yugoslav Army, which eventually turned into the Serbian Army. By the end of those conflicts, Koprivica has risen to the rank of colonel. Although he had never been found guilty of any wrongdoing, Jake guessed that just meant the man was smart enough to not get caught. Or, he was clean. A good military officer in a sea of corruption. Yet, Jake had a feeling that if the man had been clean, he had found trouble after leaving the Serbian Army and the Balkan region. Then he saw it. A disturbing fact. Koprivica had a summer home in Interlaken, Switzerland. More interesting, was the fact that his main home was in the little mountain town of Axams, Austria. A town that Jake knew quite well. Axams was just a few kilometers from Innsbruck.

Coincidences were crazy things, Jake knew. And he wasn't sure that he believed in that concept.

Jake got up and wandered back to the hotel. By now, everyone was up and about in their room.

Sirena came to Jake and kissed him quickly on the lips. "Cappuccino?"

"And apple strudel."

"You found strudel?" Johann said. The Austrian was wearing the same clothes from the night before.

"You need to find some new clothes," Jake said.

"This is Europe, Jake," Johann said. "I'm almost ripe enough for train travel."

"I'm guessing Anica is still in the shower," Jake said.

"She likes her long showers," Johann said.

"How would you know that?"

Johann turned a bit red. "From at the Polizei office. She takes her time."

Smiling, Jake said, "Hey, you are both adults."

"It's not like that," Johann said, as if he wished it were otherwise.

The door to the bathroom opened and Anica came out wearing only her bra and panties. She was built like a cross between a volleyball outside hitter and a decathlete.

"Jesus, girl. Put on some clothes," Jake said.

Johann tried not to stare, but he failed miserably.

Anica looked embarrassed and said, "I'm sorry, Uncle Jake. I didn't know you were back." She hurried into the back room and closed the bedroom door.

Sirena changed the subject. "Did you hear back from our friends yet?"

Pulling out his phone, Jake logged into his encrypted files and handed his phone to Sirena, who took a seat in a chair to read the long files.

Anica came out and gave Jake a hug. "I'm sorry," she whispered.

"Hey, I have no problem with the human body, Anica. Especially when it's as well-developed as yours. I just remember you as a scrawny little kid." He hesitated and then whispered back, "What about Johann?"

She shrugged. "I think of him as just another Polizei officer. We walk around the locker room at the station like that."

"You shouldn't," Jake said. "Coworker or not, you are extremely beautiful and have an amazing body."

"I work hard," she said.

"Obviously."

"As you know, in Austria we often sun bathe and swim topless."

He knew.

Sirena came over to Jake and Anica and said, "Leave the young girl alone. She's beautiful. If I had a body like hers, I'd show it off also."

"You are gorgeous," Anica said. "And I've seen your body. You're hot."

Jake couldn't disagree with Anica.

Johann finally chimed in from across the room. "Can we get something to eat? Strudel sounds good, but I think I need something more substantial."

"There's a full restaurant downstairs," Jake said. "Why don't you and Anica head down. We'll meet you soon."

Anica kissed Jake on both cheeks and smiled. "Don't be too long."

Once Anica and Johann left, Jake turned to Sirena and said, "What do you think?"

"Seriously? I think Anica has a smoking hot body."

"I meant about the files on my phone."

"Oh. I think we have a problem."

"How so?"

"This Caspari fellow has protection," she said. "I didn't need a classified document to tell me that. But we need to get to him fast. Once he finds out that his people in Germany and France are being brought in, he could shut down for a while."

"Right. Especially now that Fritz Giger is dead. But I have a feeling it was Caspari's men who did that."

"Why would they kill him?"

"As I mentioned last night, I'm guessing Caspari had the man's house bugged."

"Right. And they heard us talking with Giger, knowing he had given us the names of Caspari and Koprivica. They're shutting down loose ends."

"I believe this to be true," Jake said. "But it doesn't seem to make good business sense, since Giger ran so many trucks across Europe."

Sirena shrugged and shook her head. "Not everything makes sense in this world."

Yeah, Jake was infinitely aware of that fact. "Unless, Caspari plans to keep Giger's trucks in play despite the death of the Swiss man."

"Which brings us to another Serb," she said. "What do you think of the info on Koprivica?"

"You know that Axams is a small town near Innsbruck," Jake said.

"I do now. Do you think he's the man at the top?"

"That would be my guess."

She paced back and forth and finally said, "Do we go right to the top? Or should we start with Caspari?"

Jake had been considering his options since he first read the background on these men in the Weinplatz outside the hotel. "I hate to say it, but I think we should stick with the Italian. After all, his men were probably responsible for the death of Fritz Giger last night."

"And those who chased us around Zurich," Jake said.

"What do you think we should do?" she asked.

"I don't want to, but I think we should split up."

"But I thought we were doing all right," she mocked.

"You know what I mean."

She smiled. "I know. But those two are a bit raw."

"I agree. We'll have to split them up. You take one and I'll take the other."

"I could take Anica," she said. "We could head back to Innsbruck. She knows the Serbian community."

"That could be the problem. Last time she was there, they tried to kill her. She could be burned for undercover work there."

"You're right. So, I guess I'm with Johann. He is kind of cute."

"Don't get any ideas of taking on a young lover."

"You too."

"Anica? She's like a niece to me."

"But she isn't."

Sirena had a point, but Jake knew she was kidding. There was no way that he could ever think of making love to Anica.

"Is this going to be a problem?" he asked.

"No." She moved in close and kissed him on the lips. "I'm just busting your balls." She grabbed him there now and squeezed down on his groin, but in a delicate way. "You know the two of them probably think we're doing it right now. That's why we need the alone time."

"Maybe we shouldn't disappoint them." He kissed her now and she embraced him tightly.

19

After eating and checking out of the Zurich hotel, the four of them met outside at the cars. Johann got behind the wheel of his Audi and Jake met Sirena by the passenger door.

"Don't move on the Serb," Jake said. "Just gather intel. And be careful. This Jack-off fellow is dangerous."

"It's Jakov," Sirena said, smirking.

"Jack-off Jakov. Whatever. Just surveil the guy and his organization."

"Got it," Sirena said. Then she hugged Jake and kissed him passionately on the lips. "What about the Italian?"

"We'll let the situation dictate our response," he said.

"I've heard that before." She opened the door and sat down.

Jake leaned in and glared at Johann. "Don't do anything stupid."

"Yes, sir," Johann said.

"Do what Sirena tells you to do."

Johann nodded and then started the engine.

Jake closed the door and watched the Audi pull away. Then he looked back and saw Anica sitting in the passenger seat of their rental BMW. He got in and looked at her.

"I'm ready," she said. "By the way, you two are great together."

He turned over the engine. "We're keeping it casual. Whatever the hell that means."

"Where first?"

"The airport," Jake said. "We need to trade this car out for another one."

"Why?"

"The men last night, those that chased us, know this car."

"Good point."

Jake used his Austrian passport to trade out the BMW for a new Alpha Romeo Giulia Quadrifoglio. He couldn't help thinking about his first real love, Toni Contardo, who used to own these hot Italian cars. In reality, though, he was impressed by more than 500 horsepower and zero to sixty in less than four seconds. The car topped out at just under 200 mph. Just in case he ran across someone who wanted to try to follow them again.

"Is this one of those mid-life cars?" Anica asked Jake as he ran through the shift paddles.

"Maybe. I'll probably get speeding tickets in the parking lot."

The problem with going to find the Italian, Giovanni Caspari, is that he owned two houses—one in Lake Como, Italy and the other in Lucerne, Switzerland. Lucerne was less than an hour south of Zurich, so they went there first.

"I don't recommend a flashy red car like this for surveillance," Jake said, as he slowed the car and exited the autobahn ramp for central Lucerne.

"I understand," Anica said. "But it is nice on the autobahn. Caspari's business office is right down by the lakefront."

Lucerne sat on Lake Lucerne, and as far as Jake was concerned, it was one of the most beautiful places on the planet, with high mountains all around.

"This is stunning," Anica said.

"It's like a smaller Innsbruck."

"I could live here."

Jake parked in the old town area on the street adjacent to where the river Reuss drained from Lake Lucerne.

"I need to buy a few things," she said. "Could we just be tourists for a while."

"What do you need?"

"Clothes. Shirts, underwear."

"I saw your underwear this morning," Jake said. "You could carry a couple of those in your small purse."

She slapped him on the arm. "Jake. That's not nice."

"Alright. I guess I could use a few things also."

"Maybe a thong?" She smiled at him.

"In my day, Anica, thongs were worn on your feet to the beach."

They got out and walked down the street into the old town, like a father and a daughter, or an older gentleman and his trophy girlfriend. Let them guess, Jake thought.

After a short shopping excursion, they ate lunch outdoors in a small square with a view of Caspari's office on the second floor of an old building. This was prime real estate for an office that did not rely on tourists or the heavy foot traffic of this pedestrian zone. As far as Jake could tell, nobody was coming or going from the place. He guessed that Caspari owned the office for the view of the lake and the mountains.

"Now what?" Anica asked.

"If Caspari was here, you would see some signs of it. Like security personnel."

"The woman working in the office left just long enough to grab some food and bring it back upstairs," she observed.

"What else do you see?"

"Is this a test, Jake?"

"Maybe."

"You mean the security cameras?"

"What about them?"

She shrugged. "He has them. What else?"

"When the woman passed by the cameras, she looked at them and then her watch."

"Okay."

"That tells me that she suspects her boss is always watching her. Those cameras have motion sensors linked to a smart phone. Any motion sends a notice to the owner that someone is there, which they can view in real time. There's also two-way sound capability. And all of this loads to the cloud, so you can't thwart it by going inside and destroying a recording device."

"How do you know this?"

"Because I've owned the same model as those for various properties." He pulled out his phone and opened an app. Then he clicked a button and turned the phone for Anica to see a beautiful ocean view.

She smiled. "What is this camera protecting?"

"Nothing. I put in an extra one to view the ocean while away from The Azores."

Anica handed the phone back. "I will have to come to visit sometime. I've never been there."

"Any time." He put his phone away and said, "But the cameras are why we haven't gone up to the office. We'll tip our hand to Caspari. He'll know we're coming for him."

"Then what can we do?"

"Wait. I'm normally not an overly patient guy. But I've learned over the years to kick back and wait sometimes. It could save a lot of time and effort."

"I'm still confused," she said.

"Periodically, I work for a man who runs the largest communications company in Europe," Jake said. "He has access to certain things that most law enforcement agencies don't even have, including cloud-based storage."

"Isn't that illegal?"

Jake smiled and waved his hand. "Not entirely. But sometimes it takes special measures to catch the bad guys."

"But where do we draw the line, Jake?"

"Good versus evil. They're transporting drugs into Europe, which brings with it much more crime. Plus, the human trafficking problems. We don't know who they're bringing in."

"They are people trying to escape bad situations," she said.

"I know. Most of them are probably just that. But I'm worried about the one or two or ten who are here to do harm. We've seen this across Europe. Aren't you working at Europol for that exact reason?"

"Yes, of course. I just feel sorry for those trying to escape war and horrible situations. I was one of those people."

"You were a child, Anica. You had lost your parents. You were completely dependent on the kindness of strangers."

"Like you."

"I didn't do much," Jake admitted.

"You saved my life. I owe you everything."

"I saw a problem that I could fix and I did what I could."

"You have been helping me all along," she said, a tear forming in her right eye, which she wiped away with the back of her hand. "I know you helped me become a Polizei officer."

"You did that on your own, Anica." He touched her hand delicately.

"You taught me how to save and invest for the future."

"Alright, I did that. But that was just logical guidance."

Jake's phone suddenly buzzed, so he checked to see who had texted him. It was from his friends at the communications company with the information he needed.

"Is that important?" she asked.

"I think so." He opened his app and logged in with this new information. Once he did this, he could see everything. He saw multiple locations, with many cameras at each place. Jake could now look at real time images, along with historical motion events. Finding the Lucerne office, Jake swiped the motion sensors off on four cameras. Then he turned the phone to Anica.

She glanced across the square at the office. "Do you have access to his cameras?"

"Let's just say the cloud is not as secure as most would like to believe. Let's go."

"Where?"

"I shut off the cameras to Caspari's office. Now we can go in and ask a few questions."

Jake smiled at the cameras he had turned off as he passed them, and went into the second level office. It was very small and tidy, like most German, Austrian or Swiss offices. There were no loose papers anywhere, other than a few on the small desk used by the only person in the office—a woman in her mid-thirties.

"*Buona sera come stai? Sto cercando un buon amico* Giovanni."

The young woman looked confused. "My Italian is not very good," she said in German.

Jake switched to that language and asked again to see his good friend Giovanni.

The Swiss woman seemed hesitant. Finally, she said, "I'm afraid he is not in today. He should be back on Monday."

Jake feigned disappointment and said, "Too bad. We were to meet here today. I thought we had an appointment. Is he at his home in Lake Como?"

"I can't say."

Or, she wouldn't say. That's what Jake guessed she would say. He thanked her for her time and left with Anica at his side. Once they got away from the office building, along the river, Jake sat on a park bench and pulled out his phone. First, he turned the security cameras back on. Then, he called his contact as the Spanish communications company.

"What's going on?" Anica asked. "I thought you would press that woman a little harder for information."

"That wasn't my intention," he said, while he waited on the line for his information.

"You are. What's the English word for it? An enigma?"

Jake raised a finger as he listened to his contact. Then he thanked the person and cut the call. "Got it."

"Got what?"

"As soon as we left the office, as suspected, the young lady made a call to her boss, Giovanni Caspari. She called his cell phone and spoke for only three minutes. But it was long enough for our friends to track his cell phone to his location."

Anica was speechless.

Jake got up. "Are you ready for a little drive?"

"To where? Lake Como?"

"Nope. Interlaken."

She got up and whispered loudly to Jake. "That's not legal."

He shrugged. "Neither is what Caspari is doing. Sometimes you have to stretch the rules a little to catch the bad guys."

"I can't do that," she said.

Turning to Anica, Jake said, "Not officially. And you didn't do anything. I did. Now, let's go have a talk with this Italian."

20

Innsbruck, Austria

It took Sirena and Johann a little more than four hours to travel from Zurich to Innsbruck, where they went to his apartment in the northside of the city. Johann lived in a three-hundred-year-old three-story house with a beautiful view of the Alps to the south, including the Olympic ski jump. Johann's apartment on the top level had a small balcony, where Sirena stood now gazing at the city below.

She wondered where Jake was now. Since they got together months ago, they had not been apart for long. Their relationship had reached a nice level, she thought. Yet, she wasn't sure where they were going, if anywhere. And that didn't seem to matter to either of them.

Johann came out carrying two bottles of a local pilsner.

She accepted a bottle and they toasted before taking a refreshing drink.

"What's the plan?" Johann asked.

"I just got a text from Jake saying they found out Caspari was in Interlaken. They're on their way there now."

"Nice place," Johann said.

"Never been there."

"The shops are ridiculous. Rolex and Cartier. But the city is situated beautifully in the shadow of the Jungfrau, Eiger and Mönch."

"Innsbruck isn't so bad, either," she said, pointing her beer out to the Alps.

"I agree. I don't think I could live anywhere else."

"What do you think of Anica?"

He got a bit nervous with this question. "She is a great Polizei officer."

"Not bad to look at either."

Johann raised his brows as he delayed with a sip of beer. "She is very pretty," he finally said.

"How long have you been in love with her?"

"What?"

She smiled. "It's pretty obvious."

"Is it?"

"Have you dated?"

He shook his head. "People don't really date anymore. They hang out and hook up."

"And you and Anica?"

Johann shrugged. "We hang out once in a while. But not to the hooking up part."

"But you'd like to."

"You've seen her body. She keeps herself in amazing shape."

"But you seem to want more than just a hook up with her."

"She's not like other women in Innsbruck. She doesn't just hook up with men. She doesn't seem to have time."

"Why not?"

"I don't know. She's either working out or studying. She speaks five or six languages. Anica is very dedicated to her work."

Sirena drank her beer and wondered if Johann could have been talking about her in her younger years, where she was too busy to establish or maintain a relationship. "Eventually we all get to a point in life where we need something more, Johann."

"Are you speaking from personal experience?"

"I'm afraid so."

"But we're still young."

"Hey."

He turned bright red. "I didn't mean it that way."

"Shut up and get me another beer."

Johann gladly went off to the kitchen area off of the main living room.

Sirena followed him in and took a seat in a chair with a nice view of the mountains.

He came back with two more beers, setting both on the coffee table next to a large map of the city and surrounding area. Johann sat down and pointed to an area on the map. "This is where Jakov Koprivica lives in Axams. It's not far from here."

"Isn't Axamer Lizum the ski resort that hosted the Olympics?"

"Yes. Most of the races were there in both sixty-four and seventy-six."

"What have you told Sabine Bauer about Jakov Koprivica."

"Nothing. Why?"

"You do report to her," Sirena said.

"She is the Tirol Polizei boss," Johann said.

"That's not what I asked." She stared at him critically.

"What are you implying?"

"Well, we found a possible head of a large criminal organization in Tirol, and I would expect you to inform your people of this fact."

"One would think so, yes."

"But?"

Johann simply stared at her now.

She finished it for him. "But you don't trust your own Polizei."

"For the most part I do," he said, taking a drink of beer but keeping his eyes penetrating her.

"You think Jakov Koprivica has eyes in your office?"

Johann shrugged. "Maybe. I just don't know."

Perhaps that was why Sabine Bauer had come to Jake for help in the first place, she thought. "What seems to be the problem?"

"I don't know. Just a feeling. Only a few people on our end knew about the meeting between Anica and her Serbian contact. Of course, we know what happened there."

"Not to mention the drive-by shooting that could have killed us," she provided.

"Exactly."

She lifted her beer toward him and said, "*Prosit.*"

They ticked their bottles together and then drank.

"Where do we go from here?" he asked.

"I think we can trust Sabine," she said. "But we don't know if her communications have been compromised. So, better to keep her in the dark about Jakov Koprivica until we have something solid to give her."

"I agree."

"We'll need to do some discreet surveillance of the man and his operation," Sirena said. "I'm waiting to get a more detailed intelligence file on the man from another source. In the meantime, we can pull up some data on his current properties in Tirol."

Johann smiled. "I did that as soon as we got here." He slid his laptop across the table and opened it, bringing up saved files. "This is his house in Axams. In Austria, we must submit plans to the government for approval. They must meet style parameters, of course. Along with meeting environmental impact. Jakov Koprivica built his house on the edge of Axams five years ago. It is actually a main house and two smaller buildings. According to the plans, he said he would rent the other buildings for vacationers. Skiers in the winter and hikers and bikers in the summer."

"Interesting. Is there any record of him actually doing so?"

"No. Not according to his taxes."

"Then my guess is he's using those other buildings to either store something or someone."

"Perhaps migrants temporarily."

"It's possible." She checked the time on her phone. "We need to rest for a while before heading there for the evening."

"What do Americans call it? A stake out? We'll need donuts and coffee."

"Very funny, Johann. But this body is not fueled by donuts. We'll need meat and water. Preferably jerky. Protein stops hunger."

Johann ran his hand across the map and said, "If we sit on this road that leads up the mountain, we'll have an unobstructed view of the house. I have binoculars."

"Alright. As long as I have cell service in Axams, we can wait for my intel there. Let's go. I'd like to get there before dark."

While Johann packed up a few things in a bag, Sirena texted Jake to let him know her plan. She also relayed Johann's concern about a possible leak at the Polizei. Of course, Jake had already suspected this possibility when he questioned Sabine Bauer's motivation.

Just before heading out the door, Jake texted her back, saying he had just gotten to Interlaken.

21

Interlaken, Switzerland

The city of Interlaken sat in a small strip of land between two lakes, Lake Thun to the west and Lake Brienz to the east. Running through the city was the Aare River. Jake knew there were few cities in the world that could rival Interlaken for pure beauty. She was like a young girl in her prime, with perky breasts and a butt like that of an Olympic sprinter. Yeah, she was a sight to see. To truly enjoy her, though, one needed enough money for admission. Hotels were pricy. Real estate outrageous. Jake would live here if it weren't for its over-the-top pomposity. Plus, he didn't really get along with the wealthy, other than his Spanish benefactor, who had built his business from nothing.

Jake and Anica had gotten to Interlaken hours ago, and despite the proximity of this city to Innsbruck, she had never been to this mountain town of some 6,000 residents. She was immediately smitten.

They had checked into a nice old hotel in the center of the city, a block from Höheweg, where the swanky hotels sat. Jake wanted to stay away from the higher-end hotels, knowing Giovanni Caspari was staying just two blocks down Höheweg at a six-hundred dollar a night spa hotel.

Having knowledge of the location of Caspari had been important, but then Jake had found the man's actual hotel and room number.

Now, comm units in their ears, Jake and Anica lingered in the lobby of the hotel where Caspari was staying. Jake was currently at a small bar with a view of the front desk, the concierge stand, and the front entrance, where a uniformed doorman did the job that a sensor and automatic door could do.

Anica was speaking with the concierge folks, flipping through brochures and generally flirting with a younger man.

"I think the man is gay, Anica," Jake whispered into her ear through the comm.

She ignored him and continued asking about good restaurants.

Jake sipped on a Cuban rum and coke. They didn't have a good, aged rum, so this was a compromise. Crap, he thought. Had he become one of those pompous assholes who stayed at hotels like this?

He turned his head for a second, and when he turned back toward the front entrance, he saw the two men in suits come out of the bank of elevators. They stuck out here for two reasons. First, their suits were off-the-rack and didn't fit well. And second, Jake could see bulges where the men kept their weapons.

"Here we go," Jake said. "Two men in suits. Wrap it up."

Jake threw down enough money to cover his drink, with a marginal European tip, and then casually walked out toward the lobby. As he got closer to Anica, the target came out of the elevator with a younger woman on his arm.

Giovanni Caspari was a distinguished Italian man in his mid-fifties, his silver and black hair long and flowing nearly to his shoulders. His gray suit was as Italian as this man, and probably cost several thousand Euros.

Coming up behind Anica, Jake kissed her on the cheek and smiled. "Let's go, dear," he said softly in her ear.

She thanked the men, who looked extremely disappointed, and walked arm-in-arm with Jake toward the front door.

"We need to separate him from his muscle," Jake said.

"How?"

Good question.

They lucked out. Instead of getting into a car to drive somewhere, Caspari and his date had decided to walk. Jake had banked on this, knowing that the hotel was within easy walking distance of dozens of great restaurants.

Caspari and the young woman strolled together, while the two security personnel kept pace at least ten steps behind them.

Jake and Anica fell in about a half a block back from them.

In a couple of blocks, Caspari and his entourage turned down *Jungfraustrasse*, the main pedestrian shopping district of Interlaken. Here, the street became narrower, and Jake knew the area well. He had been here many times in the summer and winter, where he had skied Grindelwald. Luckily, there was a bit of chill in the air and that might have kept some pedestrians at home, making it easier to keep track of Caspari.

"He's going into the Bierhaus," Anica said.

"Good," Jake said. "We might be able to get in close to them. Remember, you're my young girlfriend, but might be interested in something more Italian."

"I don't know if I can do this," she said.

"It's just acting."

She squeezed down on his arm as they entered the bar. Inside, the place was nearly packed to capacity. High copper ceilings had fans swirling, sucking smoke up from patrons. The two security men split up, one on each side of the room with a direct view of each other and Caspari and guest, who were at the end of the bar trying to get a drink.

A group of three women were about to vacate a table, so Jake asked if they could take it.

"Hang onto this table," Jake said to Anica. "I'll get us a couple of beers."

Jake nuzzled in behind Caspari and his girlfriend, listening to them speak in Italian.

"This is crazy," Jake said in German.

Caspari turned to Jake and said, "This is Friday night at the Bierhaus." His German was nearly flawless.

The young woman with Caspari glanced at Jake nervously.

Jake said, "Who do you have to kill to get a beer?"

Caspari laughed. "That is what I was thinking."

Jake looked back at Anica and gave her a thumbs-up. "At least we got a table."

"Is that your wife?" Caspari asked.

"No. Girlfriend."

"Lovely."

"We are both blessed," Jake said, smiling and glancing at Caspari's guest.

"German?" Caspari asked.

"Austrian." Jake reached his hand out and said, "Karl Konrad."

"Italian," Caspari said, shaking Jake's hand. "Giovanni Caspari. This is my friend, Maria."

Jake shook the young woman's hand. She was reluctant and weak with her grasp.

"And your friend?" Caspari asked.

Turning toward Anica, Jake said, "Ute. We have two extra chairs. Would you like to join us?"

Caspari didn't even ask his girlfriend. He simply said, "Of course."

"Maria could take a seat while we get the beers," Jake said.

The Italian woman was about to say something, but decided to take Jake up on his offer. She wandered to the table and shook hands with Anica. Jake could hear their conversation in his comm unit, but he tried to ignore it while he spoke with Caspari.

The bartender finally came to their end of the bar and Caspari ordered four beers.

Then Caspari turned back to Jake and said, "Looks like we both like them younger."

"Maria is beautiful," Jake said.

"So is Ute. She doesn't really look German or Austrian, though."

Jake shrugged. "I believe she has some Balkan blood. Does Maria not speak German?"

"She speaks some," Caspari said. "She's not very talkative. Very contemplative."

"Nothing wrong with that," Jake said. "As long as she's good in bed."

Caspari smiled. "There is no doubt about that."

Their beers came and Caspari paid with a large bill, giving the man incentive to keep them coming. Then Jake and the Italian went to their table. Anica and the other woman were speaking Italian, seeming to get along. But this Maria was holding back, not wanting to give up any information about herself. Anica, on the other hand, was making up one hell of a legend for herself. She had mostly been a student for the past ten years, learning languages and culture—not exactly lies, but Anica had done all of this on her own time.

Maria, other than her native Italian, spoke Spanish, French, English, and German.

They drank three beers together before Maria said she needed to go. She was prone to migraines, and a bad one was coming on now.

Jake and Anica watched as Caspari and Maria left. Moments later, their security men drifted out after them, with one staring Jake down as if he wanted to kill him.

Alone at the table now, Jake let out a heavy breath and said, "Well? What do you think?"

"I think Caspari couldn't keep his eyes off of my chest."

"I noticed that. I didn't know if I should punch the man or applaud his good taste."

"Jake." She slapped his arm.

"I'm sorry. I'm just being a dude. What else?"

Anica held back and shook her head.

"What?"

"This will sound conceited. But I think Maria was more into me than Caspari."

"Good observation. I was thinking the same thing. She's not as she seems. Let's head back to our hotel."

The night air had gotten even chillier. Anica held onto Jake even tighter as they made their way along the pedestrian zone of *Jungfraustrasse*.

Ahead, the street angled to the right, and Jake felt something wasn't right. He saw a man for a second, but then he scooted down a side street.

"Did you see that," Anica whispered.

"Yeah. There's another man following us."

"The security guards?" she asked.

"I doubt it. They would stick with Caspari. Get your gun ready." Jake zipped his leather jacket down for easy access to his Glock.

As they came closer to the side street where the man had disappeared, Jake had his gun in his hand, but still inside his jacket. He slowed their pace and stopped at the edge of the building.

Jake swiveled and aimed his gun at the man following them.

Startled, the man was stuck with his own hand inside his jacket.

"Slowly remove your hand," Jake said in German.

Nothing.

So, Jake repeated himself in Italian. But the man didn't budge. Jake was sure the guy understood both languages.

Anica pulled her gun and stepped around the corner, finding herself in a standoff with another man pointing his gun at her.

The man with his hand still in his jacket said, "Please, put your guns down. We are with INTERPOL."

22

Axams, Austria

Sirena and Johann had gotten to a position on the road leading up the mountain to the ski resort just as darkness rolled across the Alps. Their Audi was nestled among a group of trees with a stone wall alongside a pull-off that allowed for a view of the city of Innsbruck in the distance. They had been there for hours now, watching what they had started to call a compound owned by Serbian immigrant Jakov Koprivica. The newer house was a two-story chalet style home with a balcony running along most of the second story. The place fit in perfectly with the rest of the town in the shadow of Innsbruck. The other two buildings were more like log cabins that foresters would use in remote locations in the Alps.

Since the two of them had been watching, there had been no movement around the two smaller buildings. But the main house had a security presence, with roving guards periodically moving around outside. To the casual observer, these men could have been simply out for a stroll and a smoke. Sirena knew better.

She had not heard from Jake in hours, which wasn't unusual. It wasn't like he needed a babysitter. Sirena sat in the passenger seat of Johann's Audi, observing the compound with binoculars.

"What are you thinking?" Johann asked.

Good question. "I don't like this."

"What's not to like. We have meat and cheese and water. What more could we need?"

"I'm not a sit still kind of woman," she revealed, and then glanced away from the binoculars for a moment.

"You like to take action."

She put the binoculars to her eyes again and said, "I would like to take Jakov Koprivica for a ride up into the mountains for a little talk."

"I won't ask you how you know what you know about him," Johann said. "But perhaps this is enough for our Polizei to bring him in for questioning. Maybe the World Court would like to prosecute him."

That was the problem, she knew. The Mossad had given her information off the record. They had called the reliability near one hundred percent, but they also had no direct evidence. According to her source, Jakov Koprivica had been heavily involved in a work camp during the war that used rape as a tool to make the locals comply with their orders. And these women were from both sides of the conflict. Koprivica was an equal opportunity abuser.

"The Hague would require witnesses to come forward," Sirena said. "Even with war, there is a statute of limitations on rape. He would need to be charged with murder and crimes against humanity."

"That was a long time ago," Johann said.

"Men like Koprivica don't change, Johann. My guess is that he is up to his old tricks."

"What do you mean?"

"If he is smuggling refugees into Austria, I'll bet he is taking advantage of the women. These women would be in no position to complain. They are powerless."

"With all of the problems with immigrants recently, our government has nearly shut down all migrants coming in to Austria."

She laughed. "That's what guys like Koprivica thrive on. But we need to catch him in the act. Human trafficking is only one part of his business. They've already found drugs in the Konstanz warehouse, along with the migrants. But I'll bet they're also into weapons sales and smuggling."

"How long do we stay here?"

"How hard is it to get a wire on this guy's house?" she asked.

"Not easy," Johann said. "We must have solid cause to do so."

"If we had cause, we wouldn't need a tap on his phone."

"He doesn't have a traditional phone. Just a cell phone."

"We have that covered," she said. "But he could have a number of disposable phones, or even a secure SAT phone."

"We could just go down and talk with the man."

"That would be a mistake. We don't want him to know that we know about his existence. At least not until we get more on him."

"Or until Jake and Anica get here," Johann said. "How are they doing?"

She took her eyes away from the binoculars and shifted her stare at the young Polizei officer. "You really like her, don't you?"

"Anica is a good friend." Johann stopped, something obviously on his mind.

"What is it?"

"I don't understand her relationship with Jake."

"She was a vulnerable young orphan who came to him for help in a dire moment in her life. Jake helped her get placed with a Tirol Polizei family, who helped raise her. Anica is obviously someone who remembers those who have helped her in the past. It's an admirable quality."

"I see. So, there's nothing physical with them?"

Sirena punched Johann in the arm. "Don't be an idiot. She's like a niece to Jake."

"But, still."

"You obviously don't know jack about Jake. The man is an Eagle Scout."

"What is that?"

"You have Boy Scouts in Austria."

"Yes, of course. I understand. He's a straight shooter. Honorable."

"That's right." Sirena saw a car coming up the mountain. "Is that her?"

Johann grabbed the binoculars from Sirena and he focused on the approaching car. "That's her."

"Is she alone?"

"Looks like it. That's what you told her, right?" Johann handed the binoculars back to her.

"Yeah."

The BMW cruised by them slowly. Then the driver turned off her lights, pulled a U-turn, and parked behind them. The woman climbed into the back seat of the Audi and leaned forward between the two front bucket seats.

Kriminal Hauptkommisar of Tirol, Sabine Bauer, asked, "Why am I here?"

Sirena turned to her and said, "You don't trust everyone in your office." It wasn't a question.

"Why do you say that?" Sabine asked.

"Not exactly a denial," Sirena observed.

"You're about as confounding as Jake Adams."

"I've been told," Sirena said. "But it was a simple deduction. You wouldn't have flown all the way to The Azores and convinced Jake to come to Austria if you trusted your Polizei officers to find Anica."

Sabine's eyes shifted out through the windshield. "I think we might have a problem. And I knew that Jake could be trusted."

Finally, the truth, Sirena thought. "Okay. Here's what we've got." She explained what they had discovered in France and German so far, along with Jake and Anica tracking the Italian in Switzerland. Sirena finished by explaining the link to the man living down the mountain, the Serb, Jakov Koprivica.

"He's never come up on our radar," Sabine said.

Sirena explained all of the intel she had on the guy.

"That's terrible," Sabine said, "But I'm not sure we can bring him in based on this information."

"That's why we're here."

"When those in our office knew about Anica working undercover to infiltrate a possible Serbian organization, she was nearly killed."

"That's why you're going to keep this from your people for now," Sirena said.

23

Interlaken, Switzerland

All four of them had put their guns away and walked to a large park along Höheweg. A number of high-end hotels were lit up brightly, electricity obviously free in this opulent city.

Jake had verified the credentials of the two men, but they would not talk until they were sure they were far away from the pedestrian zone.

Once they were in a secluded area, Jake turned to the lead agent and said in English, "Why were you following us?"

"Because you were about to compromise our investigation into Giovanni Caspari," the Italian said.

"Maria is INTERPOL," Jake surmised.

"Yes, she is with us."

Anica chimed in. "You make her sleep with that man?"

"No. She volunteered, knowing she would have to do certain things. She is a professional."

"If she wasn't before, she is now," Anica said, shaking her head.

"Caspari is a bad man," the Italian said. "He is responsible for human trafficking, smuggling drugs and weapons through Italy. Who knows what else?"

"Why is INTERPOL investigating instead of the Italians?" Anica asked.

Jake took this one. "Caspari has probably paid off certain Polizia officials."

"And politicians. Border patrols are paid in cash through an intermediary. We know Caspari is responsible, but we have not caught him directly." The INTERPOL man hesitated long enough to check out Anica and then turned back to Jake. "We understand she is Austrian Polizei working for Europol. But who are you?"

"A concerned citizen," Jake said.

"According to our people, you checked into your hotel under the name Karl Konrad, with an Austrian passport. But you do not seem to have much of a German accent."

"I studied English in America as an exchange student," Jake explained.

"I see. But why are you following and engaging Giovanni Caspari?"

Jake expected this question. "That's classified."

"So, you are not just a concerned citizen," the Italian said. "What do you have on Caspari?"

"Not enough," Jake said. "I'll tell you what. You give me something, and I'll return the favor."

"We can't discuss an ongoing investigation."

They could go in circles like this all evening, Jake thought. "Let me see your identification."

"Why?"

Jake waved his hand and INTERPOL pulled out his ID. Jake took a quick photo on his phone and attached it to a text to a friend. It took just five uncomfortable minutes waiting in the cool night air for Jake to get a return text from his friend at INTERPOL.

The text read, 'The guy is legitimate. One of the good guys.'

"Alright," Jake said. "You check out. Did you hear about the bust in Konstanz?"

"Yes, of course."

"That was Anica. Goran Goluža gave up Caspari."

The INTERPOL officer nodded his head. "We knew about a potential link to Goluža. We believe this organization is operating in every European country, but we have not been able to find the top leader."

Jake didn't want to mention Jakov Koprivica. At least not yet. Not while Sirena was checking into the man. He said, "It could be a decentralized structure with a number of top leaders."

"A consortium," INTERPOL surmised.

"Perhaps."

"Well, this is a European law enforcement matter," the INTERPOL officer said.

Jake shifted his head to Anica and said, "She is with Austrian Polizei and affiliated with Europol."

"This is Switzerland," he said. "Not a member of the European Union."

Now Anica chimed in. "Then I'm sure you have run your operation through the Swiss Polizei."

The INTERPOL man fought for his words, but he had nothing for a full minute. Finally, he said, "We followed Caspari from Lake Como, and have not had time to coordinate our efforts with the Swiss. What about you?"

Jake didn't need to tell this man anything, but he decided to at least keep things civil. "We are simply gathering intelligence for now. Once we get enough information, we'll bring in the Swiss."

The INTERPOL man's phone buzzed and he pulled it from his front pocket. He swore in Italian and switched to English to say, "We must go." The two INTERPOL officers headed off toward the hotel where Maria was staying with Caspari.

"Is it Maria?" Jake asked.

The men stopped and turned to Jake. "Why do you say that?"

"Because she seemed nervous," Jake said. "As if she thought Caspari might know about her."

"She sent her distress code," he said.

"Caspari has at least two security guards," Jake said. "We can help."

INTERPOL nodded and hurried across the park toward the high-end hotel at the edge.

Jake and Anica followed the two INTERPOL officers into the hotel lobby to the bank of elevators. They went up to the fourth floor together. When the doors opened, Jake stepped out first, saw the two security guards, and pulled his gun when he saw they were aiming their guns at him.

Shots rang out in the corridor.

With just a second to react, Jake scooted back into the elevator and simultaneously pulled his gun. "Two shooters," Jake said. Then he went low around the elevator door and shot twice at the men.

They returned fire with a dozen shots.

The Italian INTERPOL officers looked hesitant to Jake, as if this were the first gunfight they had experienced.

Glancing around the door, Jake saw that the two men had been joined by a third man. Caspari. And they were rushing down the hallway toward the emergency stairwell.

"They're heading toward the stairs," Jake said, and then rushed out the door and after the men.

One of the men turned and fired at Jake. Vectoring to the right, Jake shot three times, dropping the man to his knees. But he must have only hit the man in the leg, because his friend was able to help him to the stairs.

Hurrying to the hotel room, Jake stopped and waited for the INTERPOL officers to catch up. Anica was behind them.

"Do you need to go after them?" Jake asked. "I hit one of them."

"We check on Maria first," the INTERPOL man said.

The hotel room door was locked, so the Italian shoved his shoulder into the door. It wouldn't budge.

Jake pushed the man out of the way and kicked the door alongside the handle. The frame gave way enough for Jake to shove his shoulder into the door and smash it inward against the wall.

Moving quickly into the room, his gun out in front, Jake swept through the opulent old hotel room. He found Maria at the far end of the room at the edge of the balcony door. She was bloody and not moving.

The INTERPOL men were now upon Jake, and both men gasped when they saw Maria's beaten face. One checked the woman's pulse, while the other got on his phone and called for help.

"No pulse," INTERPOL said. He immediately tried to perform CPR.

Based on the amount of blood and the coloring of her skin, Jake knew this woman would not survive. Besides the beaten face, the woman's neck was bruised thoroughly. Someone had choked her out.

The second INTERPOL officer said an ambulance was on its way.

Jake pulled out the car keys and handed them to Anica. "Go get the Alfa."

"Why?"

"We're going after Caspari," Jake said.

She smiled. "Meet you out front in ten."

Once Anica was gone, Jake leaned down to the INTERPOL officer trying to revive Maria. "She's gone," Jake said. "Her neck is broken."

The Italian continued compressions, but asked, "How do you know?"

Jake thought back through his life and remembered the sound and look of those he had been forced to choke out and eventually break their necks. It was always a disconcerting event. "Trust me," Jake said. "I know."

The INTERPOL man stopped and sat next to the young woman. He brushed the hair away from her lifeless eyes and then tried to close her lids, but they wouldn't budge.

"Hey," Jake said. "You now have Caspari for murder. Get your ass in gear and arrest the man. Make the man talk."

INTERPOL swished his head side to side. "The Swiss will take on the murder investigation."

"Yes, but they won't have all the data if we leave now," Jake explained. "You can get the man first."

"How? They have a head start. They could be anywhere."

Jake didn't want to give away what he knew, so he said, "You know about his place in Lucerne and Como."

The man nodded his head.

Leaving the two men to wait for medical response and the Swiss Polizei, Jake casually walked out and took the elevator to the lobby. He found Anica waiting out front already with the Alfa Romeo.

He got into the passenger side and glanced at Anica.

"Is she dead?" Anica asked, and then pulled away from the curb onto the street.

"Yeah." Jake took out his SAT phone and found the app he needed.

"Where are we going?" she asked.

"Away from here for now until I get a location. This place will soon be crawling with Polizei."

"They should have heard all of those shots and got here by now."

Jake had to agree. Not a great response time. But he could finally hear sirens approaching. Interlaken was normally a sedate, tourist resort town. Prime assignment for the soon to retire or the connected, he guessed.

"Turn left ahead," Jake said.

Anica followed his order, picking up speed. "Are we getting on to the autobahn?"

"No. Follow *Grindelwaldstrasse*."

"Are we going after these men?" she asked.

Jake knew they could simply let INTERPOL and the Swiss Polizei handle Caspari and his men, but for some reason he thought he might be able to get more intel out of this man than the locals. They had rules; Jake made up his own rules.

"They stopped in Grindelwald," Jake said. "Have you been there?"

"No."

"It's a beautiful ski resort and not much else. Looks like they stopped on the outskirts of town. Let's see what this car will do on the mountain roads."

"You trust me?"

"You grew up driving through the Alps."
She smiled and hit the gas.

24

Grindelwald, Switzerland

It took them less than thirty minutes to drive up the mountain road from Interlaken to Grindelwald. Jake remembered the place from a ski vacation he had taken one winter when he lived in Innsbruck. That year he had hit nearly every major ski resort in Austria and Switzerland. The beauty of this place, unfortunately, was obscured by darkness and swirling clouds overhead.

Just as they got to the outskirts of the mountain village, Jake had found out who lived at the address where Caspari and his men had gone.

Now, they sat a couple of blocks away from the mountain chalet. GPS indicated Caspari's car was still there, but they must have put it in the garage.

"Nice place," Anica said. "Who lives there?"

"A doctor from Lucerne. A second home. The man is a surgeon."

"They're patching up the man you shot."

"Yep."

"What do we do? Should we just call the Swiss Polizei? Or INTERPOL?"

"You have authority through Europol," Jake said.

"Although Switzerland is not part of the European Union, they have agreed to cooperate with us. But they expect us to call if we know the location of a known murderer."

That's what Jake thought. But he didn't have such restrictions. "We need to talk with Caspari before he can get a lawyer and shut down an interview."

"I follow the rules, Jake," she said, a hint of desperation in her voice. She obviously didn't want to disappoint him.

"Was it standard procedure to jump in the river during a gun fight and disappear for days without contacting your office?" Jake asked. A bit harsh, he knew, but it would get his point across.

"That's not fair," she said.

"You've never explained why you disappeared."

Anica let out a heavy sigh. She bit her lower lip and shook her head. "I wasn't sure who to trust. Somehow our operation had been compromised. Besides, I was really working for Europol at the time. I was used to working with more autonomy with them."

"I guessed that much," Jake said. "Otherwise, Sabine Bauer wouldn't have flown all the way to The Azores to recruit me. She had to think there was a mole in your organization."

"Did she say that?"

"Not exactly. It was implied by her actions." Jake considered what to do. He sure as hell didn't want to get Anica in trouble with the Polizei or Europol. He also didn't want to put her in harm's way. "Alright. I'll go and recon the chalet. My guess is the doctor will be working on the guy I shot, leaving the other man and Caspari. Not much of a problem."

Jake made sure he had a full magazine in his Glock, and he added rounds he had used at the hotel from the depleted magazine. Then he shoved the gun into its holster under his left arm and started to get out.

Anica reached across and grabbed Jake's arm. "Jake. Be careful."

"I got this," he said, and then got out into the cool night air. Grindelwald sat in the shadows of the snowy glaciers of the Eiger, which Jake could see periodically when the clouds cleared.

He made it around the side of the house with the garage, skirting a row of pines. Here chalets speckled the hills of green grass, with just enough trees to provide shade in the summer. The good doctor's house was on a particularly steep section a few blocks from the train leading up the mountain to the *Kleine Scheidegg* ski area. In the summer, Grindelwald was base camp for those crazy enough to climb the north face of the Eiger.

Jake rounded the back of the house, which would have a spectacular view of the Eiger if it were not past midnight. As he suspected, the door to the walkout basement wasn't locked. He quietly went inside and slowly drew his gun. The sound of Wagner emanated from somewhere upstairs. As he slowly stepped up the stairs, he could now hear people talking. They were speaking Italian, so it was probably Caspari and his security guard.

Once on the main level, Jake stepped into the lavish home of wood and wrought iron. The chalet resembled a medieval castle, with solid stone floors and lighting of flickering fake candles.

He stopped suddenly when he realized the men were no longer talking.

A flash of movement ahead, and then a muzzle flash. Instinctively, Jake shot once and heard what had to be a body crashing into the stone floor.

When he sensed something to his left, Jake pointed his gun at Caspari. The Italian had a pocket pistol in his right hand.

"Drop the gun," Jake said, first in Italian and then in English.

Caspari smiled and said, "I will set it down. It cost me six hundred Euros." Then the man gently reached down and placed the small semi-auto handgun in the center of a stone block. "Did you shoot my man?"

Jake moved to his right until he could see the second of Caspari's men sprawled in an awkward position on the solid surface, blood seeping from his chest and pooling outward.

"He shot first," Jake said.

"At an intruder," Caspari said.

"I'm here on official business," Jake lied. "You just killed an INTERPOL officer in Interlaken. The Swiss Polizei are looking for you. By now, INTERPOL has a Red Notice out on you. So, it's not likely that you can claim I'm an intruder. You and your people had to conclude that I was law enforcement. Yet, your man still shot at me. Why did you kill Maria?"

Caspari shrugged. "The bitch lied to me for weeks."

"Tell that to the judge before he sends you to jail."

Laughing, Caspari said, "Have you seen a Swiss jail? They're like a high-end spa. Besides, she pulled a gun on me. I had no choice but to defend myself."

"Right. Stick with that story. Then why did you shoot at me as I got off the elevator?"

"That was not me. It was my overzealous security detail—both of which you have now shot."

"Where is the gimp?" Jake asked.

Caspari looked confused.

Jake said, "The guy with the bullet in his leg."

The Italian said nothing.

"Let me guess. Your friend, the doctor, the owner of this chalet, is pulling the bullet out right now. Doesn't matter. Let's go."

"Go where?"

"I'm taking you for a ride."

Just then an older gentleman in scrubs came around the corner. When he saw Jake with the gun, he stopped dead in his tracks.

In German, Jake asked, "How is our patient?"

The doctor glanced at Caspari, as if he was looking for an explanation.

"He will live," the doctor said. "I have sedated him. He will be out for hours." Then he looked at the other man on his formerly nice stone floor. "But I'm afraid he will not be alright."

Jake waved his gun at the man. "Go back to check on your patient. No need to call the Polizei. I am already here."

Without hesitation, the doctor scurried off.

"Sit down," Jake said.

Caspari moved past Jake and took a seat on a plush white leather sofa.

"And don't give me a reason to bloody the doctor's furniture," Jake said.

The Italian crossed his arms over his chest.

Jake's phone buzzed and he pulled it out to read a text from Anica. Instead of typing back, Jake called her quickly. "Yeah," Jake said in German. "Everything alright?"

"That's what I want to know," she said. "I heard shots."

Glancing at the dead guy on the floor, Jake said, "A slight misunderstanding. I'm with Caspari. He's about to tell me everything he knows."

Caspari laughed, but tried to hold it back.

Jake turned and whispered, "Take a nap. I might be here a while."

"Okay." She hung up.

Putting his phone away, Jake said, "Now, we can do this the hard way, or we can do this the ludicrous way. It's your choice. But let me explain a couple of things to you. First, I have successfully interrogated everyone from KGB spies to mafia hit men to the most zealous Islamic terrorists. You know what they all have in common?" Jake didn't expect the man to answer, so he continued. "Everyone talks. It's the nature of man. We have this great desire to live. And to live without pain or disfigurement. For instance, I could break every finger and toe on your body. That would be painful. I could cut out your eyes and you would never be able to enjoy the beauty of a woman again. Or, I could cut off your manhood and you would no longer have the will to live." Jake smiled. "I know you like the ladies. Maybe that's the way to go."

Caspari shook his head. "But you are Polizei. You can't do that to me."

Jake wagged his finger at the Italian. "Not so fast. You inferred from my language that I was Polizei. A false assumption, of course. I'm not restricted by the same rules as law enforcement. That's kind of why I left government employment so long ago. Too many rules."

Now the Italian seemed to sink into the sofa like a baby in a feather bed.

"Shall we begin?" Jake asked.

25

Innsbruck, Austria

The two of them had sat outside the compound in Axams until the entire place went dark. Sirena was certain that Jakov Koprivica was a bad man, but now they had to prove it. This was always the hardest part of cases like this, she thought. During her career, she had been loaned out to the FBI for certain domestic cases that needed someone with her particular expertise. Those were never fun times. The process of long, drawn out police work did not appeal to her. She preferred to get in and get out.

She sat now on the small sofa in Johann's Innsbruck apartment near the river, working on her third beer. Johann was on number four, and seemed to be well on his way to pickle status.

He was a nice young man, she thought. Which was not her initial thought when he ducked and covered and did not fire back when those shooters tried to cut them down after she and Jake first got to Innsbruck to look for Anica. He was simply inexperienced, she concluded.

"What are you thinking?" Johann asked her.

She smiled. "Never ask a woman that, Johann. She might actually tell you."

"Is that so bad?"

"It can be. Depending on the woman."

He hesitated just long enough to take a long draw on his bottle of beer, his eyes still concentrating on her. "What about Anica?"

"What about her?" she asked. She knew what.

He shrugged.

"Have you two at least done some exploration?"

"You mean sex."

"Young people do have sex, right?"

"We're not that young."

"You're both under thirty," she said. "That's young. I have guns older than you."

They stared at each other for a long moment.

Finally, he said, "We hooked up once. But we were both quite drunk."

"So, it wasn't that satisfying."

"I was able to, but I don't think she was overly enthused by the prospect."

"Most young guys can complete the task if they're not in a coma. But for women, we like to at least be conscious."

"She was awake, but she just didn't seem that into it."

"Maybe she likes girls."

"No."

"Maybe she wants something more."

"I am above average size," Johann said. "I could show you."

"No. That's not what I meant. I'm talking about a more meaningful relationship. Also, if you show me your junk, I'll have to kick your ass. Not to mention what Jake will likely do to you."

"Good point. He's intense."

"You have no idea."

"How are they doing?" he asked.

"Nothing has changed since you heard from Anica," she said.

"What does it mean that Jake was going to have a talk with Caspari?"

She shook her head and drank down the last of her beer. Then she said, "That means Jake is usually making somebody talk. Deep interrogation."

"Will he get what we need?"

"When Jake talks with someone, that can mean a number of things. It could be a soft interrogation, where Jake simply asks innocuous questions and people spill their guts to him. Or, it could be something entirely different."

"Torture?"

"Torture never really works," she said. "It's more like enticement. The subject must know that Jake will do anything to get the information. The Polizei can't do that. The bad guys know that they have certain rules."

"And Jake has no rules," Johann concluded.

"He has rules. But, depending on the subject, those rules can be quite brutal. He won't treat Caspari like he would a terrorist. Caspari has already seen Jake shoot both of his men, killing one. So, he knows Jake will at least go that far."

"Isn't that far enough?"

"There are far worse things than dying, Johann. A bullet to the head doesn't hurt, I would suspect."

Johann lifted his nearly empty beer and said, "I'm one up on you. Would you like another?"

"Sure. I have a feeling nothing will happen tomorrow until evening."

He went to the adjoining kitchen area and brought back two beers, handing one to Sirena before sitting down. Then he asked, "Tell me about Jake Adams."

Sirena took a drink from her new beer. Then she said, "He's like the Alps. Nice to look at, but he can be very dangerous if you're not careful around him. But I'm sure you've done a background on him."

"That's the problem," Johann said. "He has an interesting status in Austria. One I've never seen before. Years ago, our president bestowed the highest honor given to civilians—the Great Golden Decoration with Star of Austria. He's also an honorary Teutonic Knight."

"I've seen his sword," she said with a smile.

"He has also been given a lifetime permit to carry a concealed handgun in Austria. Not even retired Polizei officers are allowed to do that."

She had heard Jake talk about this, but had never asked how he had achieved such high regard from those in political power in Austria.

"My guess is that more citizens in Austria wish they could keep and bear arms like their American cousins," she said.

"This is true. We make some of the best guns in the world, and ship most of those to America." He stopped long enough to drink more beer. "But with regards to Jake, I guess I want to know more about his psychology."

"Aw. The world according to Jake. If you are friends with him, he will do anything for you—including put his life on the line to protect you. But if you cross him and become his enemy. . ." She shook her head. "There's no place to hide in this world. He will find you. But he won't kill you in cold blood. From what I know of him, he has never killed anyone without provocation."

Johann leaned forward in his chair. "How many people has he killed?"

She shrugged. "I really don't know. I don't think he knows."

"Five or ten?" he asked.

"He's killed that many in one mission," she explained.

Johann sunk back into his chair again and drank more beer. "Wow. How does he live with that?"

"He sleeps like a baby," she said. "Like I said, every one of the dirtbags deserved what they got. It was either kill or be killed. He's saved my life more times than I can remember."

"So, Anica is in good hands."

"Generally."

"What does that mean?"

"Jake can't always protect those closest to him. Sometimes there's collateral damage. It's unavoidable."

"I understand."

"He's seen a lot of loss in his life," she said.

"Anica mentioned that he lost his girlfriend recently."

"It's been a while now, but that was just one. He's lost three women close to him."

"Yet, you are still with him."

"I'm not afraid of dying," she said. "I'm afraid of not living. With Jake, I feel alive every day."

He acknowledged with a vehement nod.

She drank the last of her beer and said, "This girl needs to hit the sack."

Johann looked confused.

"Go to bed," she explained.

"You can have my bed," he said. "I'll take the sofa."

"No. I only sleep in one man's bed."

"I meant nothing by that."

"I know. I'll be more comfortable out here. Besides, Jake might call."

They went through the normal ritual of pre-bed. Finally, Sirena was alone on the sofa in the darkness of Johann's living room, a few slivers of light seeping through the cracks of the Rolladen shutters. She couldn't help wondering what Jake was doing at this hour. Was he getting what he needed from the Italian? She would find out soon enough, she guessed.

26

Interlaken, Switzerland

A few miles east of Interlaken, on the south shore of Lake Brienz, Jake pulled the Alfa Romeo into a rest area. Here the mountains swept down to the shore, requiring several tunnels, and this rest area was between two of those tunnels. The sun was trying its best to cut through the swirling clouds as it poked over the mountains to the east on this early Saturday morning.

Anica slept in the passenger seat, but she woke as soon as the car came to a halt. She wiped her face and glanced at Jake. "Was I snoring?"

"No. Quiet as a mouse."

"I've heard some noisy mice."

Jake pulled out his phone and saw that his contact had sent him a text during his drive down the mountain from Grindelwald. He checked his watch and realized he was right on time, but his contact was running a little late. Jake would allow it, since his contact had gotten up early and driven from the capital of Bern.

"Who are we meeting?" she asked, and then yawned.

"An old friend."

"In law enforcement?"

"Not exactly."

"Ah. Another spy."

Jake smiled and thought about his old friend Hans Disler with the Swiss Federal Intelligence Service or FIS. They had worked together as far back as the Cold War era. But like most of the shadow warriors Jake had known over the years, they were either close to retired, retired, or dead. Now, Jake will have met Hans for the second time in just a few days—first in Zurich and now in the Swiss Alps.

He saw in his rearview mirror a Mercedes exit the highway. Since Jake had given Hans the description of his rental car, the FIS officer pulled in next to Jake and lifted his chin with a slight smile. Like the other night, Hans had a vape stick hanging out the side of his mouth.

Hans was code named The Snow Leopard, mostly because of his blond hair and a subdued birthmark on his right cheek in the shape of a cat's head. The blond hair had given way to silver now, and much of that had thinned out into a comb over.

"Is that him?" Anica asked.

"Yeah." Jake went to open the door, but hesitated. "You should probably stay out of this. Hang loose here."

"Works for me."

Jake got out and met his old friend around the back of the cars. They shook hands and turned that into a brief hug.

"You've gotten old, my friend," Hans said.

"You should talk," Jake said. "Now that I see you in the light of day, I'm wondering why your government hasn't put you out to pasture yet."

Hans shrugged and smirked. "If I wait one more year I get a higher pension." Then he turned and looked out at the lake. "The other night I mentioned buying a retirement home on a lake. I'm thinking of buying on the north side of this lake."

"How do you like working in Bern?"

"The FIS is not like working for the Strategic Intelligence Service in the old days. But Bern is much better than most of the places I've been assigned. We have more enemies at our gates."

Jake slapped his hand against the trunk of the Alfa. "I can attest to that."

"Nice car," Hans said.

"Rental. I wish it was mine. Tell me that Mercedes is a company car."

"It is. I drive an Audi SUV. We get a lot of snow here, and I have grandkids now."

Jake raised his hands. "And all this time I thought you were a bachelor. You actually found a woman to marry you. Mail order?" He shifted his glance toward the trunk of the Alfa. "You want to know what I've got for you?"

"You're a funny bastard. But mostly just a bastard." He hesitated long enough to suck on his vape stick and let out a long stream of steam. "Your message was cryptic at best," Hans finally said.

Giving the man the short version of what the Italian, Caspari, had told him that night, Jake said he would give him more once he confirmed a few details.

"And they're operating in Switzerland?" Hans asked.

"Austria, Switzerland, Germany, France and Italy," Jake said. "But more than likely every country."

"But you don't want to give me the name of those at the top. Then why should I help?"

"Because these people have compartmentalized their structure," Jake said. "Caspari only knows one rung above him." This was a lie, of course, but Jake guessed that Hans would also suspect this was the case.

Hans considered his options. "What do you want me to do with this Caspari fellow?"

"The Swiss Polizei and INTERPOL both want him for the murder of an INTERPOL agent last night in Interlaken."

"I heard about that. Are you sure this man killed her?"

"Positive. I was at the hotel last night." He left out the part about shooting one of Caspari's men at the hotel and having to kill the other one at the Grindelwald chalet. That would come out later, Jake thought.

"Let's take a look," Hans said.

Jake opened the trunk and they stared at Caspari, who was still sleeping. Sedated actually, thanks to the doctor at the chalet.

"Is he dead?"

"He's just a little tired," Jake said.

"Very few bruises. Clean work."

Jake shrugged. "I had to slap him around a little bit. But the guy seemed to understand early on that I wasn't going to listen to a bunch of crap."

"You have that impact on people, Jake."

"Hey, I'm a people person."

The two of them hauled the Italian out of the trunk and put him in the trunk of the Mercedes. Jake had gagged the Italian and taped his hands behind his back securely.

Hans pulled out his keys and stopped. "How much time do you need?"

That was a hard question to answer. "At least a few days."

"That I can do," Hans said. "I can put him in a safe house for a few days and then start my own interrogation."

"INTERPOL will eventually want him, but they're secondary to the big picture. If we play this right, we can reach the top. Caspari is a middle man at best."

"But murder is murder," Hans said. "Our Polizei will want to take him eventually."

"You guys can pass him around like a cheap whore for all I care. A week would be better."

Hans smiled. "As you know, Jake, the bureaucracy moves like a slug across broken glass."

They shook hands again and Jake watched as the Swiss FIS officer pulled out of the wayside rest area. Then he got back behind the wheel of the Alfa Romeo.

"I could have brought him in," Anica said.

"I know. You'll eventually get credit for his arrest."

"I don't care about that."

"I know. But you deserve credit. If you brought Caspari in now, he would probably spill his guts like a kid at his first confession."

"What about the wounded security guard at the doctor's house in Grindelwald?" she asked.

Jake smiled. "You slept through that. I called the local Polizei and gave them up, saying he and the doctor were linked to Maria's murder."

"Aren't you afraid the guard will say what he knows?"

"He doesn't know enough about the organization for us to worry. Caspari kept his people in the blind."

"He can identify you."

"No. He was unconscious the whole time. And the doctor isn't about to say anything. Not if he wants to keep his license."

She nodded approvingly. "I'm learning a lot from you."

"Try not to remember the bad habits," he said, and then started the engine.

"Where are we going now?"

"Caspari verified that he worked for Jack-off."

"You mean Jakov Koprivica."

"Whatever." He pulled out of the parking lot and quickly got up to speed on the highway. "I'll drive until we get breakfast. But then you'll need to let this old man get some shuteye."

She combed his hair with her fingers. "You are getting pretty gray. But it's nice. Distinguished."

"More like haggard," he said, and paddled through the gears until he hit the eighth speed.

They went through a few more tunnels until the road opened up on the way toward Lucerne.

"Let our people know we're on our way," Jake said.

27

Vaduz, Lichtenstein

It was almost 400 kilometers from Interlaken, Switzerland to Innsbruck, Austria. On a normal drive, Jake could make that run in less than three hours. But he wasn't in a hurry to get there. He had a couple of things to do to prepare for any potential encounter with Jakov Koprivica. First of all, he needed to wait for more intel on the man, and that meant contacting his old friends at the Agency. He was still waiting for them to get back with him. Second, he needed to rest his old body.

Although Anica had picked up the driving task shortly after dropping off the Italian with Jake's friend at Swiss Intel, even she had gotten sleepy on the journey. So, several times they had pulled off the road and taken naps in the car.

Now, in the capital of Lichtenstein, Jake decided to go to one of his tax haven banks and make a quick adjustment. Over the years he had opened bank accounts in Luxembourg, Switzerland, Lichtenstein, Andorra and Belize. He had added cash to those accounts in safe deposit boxes, and held certain other items that could not be traced back to him. He also had weapons stored in various locations, from storage units in Montana to Germany and Austria.

Jake had brought Anica into the bank with him, hoping to provide her with a little wisdom. The banker had just helped Jake retrieve his box and left the two of them alone in a small, private room.

"You seem to surprise me daily," Anica said.

Jake opened his medium box and glanced at her. "I've been keeping storage boxes like this for decades. I still have a Swiss account, but have gotten rid of my safe deposit box when they decided to change their banking laws a number of years ago." He would eventually need to let his son Karl know about all of his accounts in case anything happened to him. Not even Sirena knew the details of all of his accounts. Then again, she also had similar accounts. Just not as many, he guessed.

"What's the point?" she asked.

Jake pulled out a Glock 19 and dropped the full magazine into his hand. Then he cycled back the slide to make sure he had not left one in the chamber. It was clear. He shoved the magazine back into the handle and racked a round into the chamber. Then he put the gun into a specially-designed holster inside his leather jacket.

Next, he found a fat envelope and pulled out a stack of money—Euros and dollars. "This is much easier now with the Euro," Jake said. "I used to keep Marks, Shillings and Francs in here."

Peeling off a number of bills, Jake then returned the rest to the box. He rummaged through the box to remember what else he had in there, and he found a photo of himself and Toni Contardo on the Italian Riviera. Toni was wearing a white bikini, her dark olive skin in perfect contrast and her raven curly hair flowing in the wind over her strong shoulders. Jake was wearing a tight white suit, his muscles in full display. He even saw the bandage on the side of his head where he had been grazed by a bullet in an operation on an aircraft carrier. Wow. That was a long time ago, he thought.

Anica came around to his side of the table and looked at the photo. "Is that you?"

"Afraid so. Don't judge me by my shorts."

"You were hot, Uncle Jake."

"As opposed to my current state of atrophy."

"Well, you're still hot. But this. . ." She bit her lower lip. "I can see why that hot girl is with you. Who is she?"

"The mother of my son, Karl."

"You have a son?"

"Long story."

"How old is he?"

"A little younger than you."

"If he looks anything like you did back then, you should be setting me up."

He put the photo back in the box and closed it. That wasn't a bad idea, he thought. But Karl was off with the Agency working somewhere undercover.

"That would be a really good idea," Jake said. "I think you two would have a great deal in common. Like you, he speaks a number of languages."

"What does he do?" she asked.

Jake was ready for this question. "He's a diplomat with our State Department."

"I see. Do you get to see him much?"

"I saw him a couple of months ago in Iceland. Before that, we played around in the Baltic states for a while. I didn't even know of his existence until a few years ago. He was an Army officer by then."

"This woman didn't tell you? That's terrible. Give me her number and I'll call her and tell her so."

"She's dead," Jake said bluntly.

"Oh. I'm sorry."

"We know the risks when we take on assignments with our governments," Jake said. "It happens."

"So, she was with your Agency also?"

"Yes. She was once the station chief in Vienna."

Neither said a word for a while.

Finally, Anica said softly to Jake, "You were in love with her."

"I was. She was my first real love."

She put her hand on his arm. "I am so sorry."

He didn't have time to mention Anna or Alexandra, two other major losses in his life. Jake was pretty good at compartmentalizing the death of these three women. He would usually drown out that loss with vast quantities of alcohol.

Before calling the banker back in, he opened the box again and found two boxes of fifty rounds of 9mm hollow points, along with a second full magazine. With the Glock 17 he carried under his left arm, that would give him quite a bit of firepower. But the Serb would likely have submachine guns. His handguns wouldn't hold up against those.

"Let's go," Jake said. He summoned back the banker and together they locked the safe deposit box into its home on the wall. Jake would have to remember to come back and replenish this one.

They got back to the Alfa Romeo in the parking lot across from the bank, but didn't get in.

"I need something to eat," Anica said.

"I know a pizzeria about a block from here. Very good. Napoli style."

"I should watch my figure," she said, "in case you decide to introduce me to your hot son. But we have to eat."

"That's the spirit."

The two of them walked off toward the pizzeria, and Jake looked up at the swirling clouds over the mountains. That didn't look good, he thought.

•

Sitting in a VW Passat a block away, the two men watched as the man and woman moved away from the red Alfa Romeo.

The driver said to the passenger in German, "He doesn't look so dangerous."

"But he is," the passenger said. "We need to trust our intel on that."

"What's the plan?"

"Stick with him and wait for instruction."

28

Innsbruck, Austria

Sirena and Johann had spent most of the day simply wandering around the downtown of this Tirol city, finally enjoying a nice day of sunshine. But that would soon change, Sirena knew, since reports indicated that a storm was brewing and heading in from the Alps. They would even get some snow at higher elevations. Down in the valley around Innsbruck, precipitation would come in rain. The wind could make things even worse.

She had been glad to get a text from Anica earlier that morning saying they would be driving back from Switzerland. With Jake driving, she would have guessed they would be here by now, but there was still no word of their arrival.

The two of them sat at a coffee shop near the Inn River. Johann was wearing a hat and sunglasses, in case one of his colleagues with Polizei recognized him.

"You look like the Unabomber," Sirena said.

"The what?"

"Never mind."

Her phone suddenly buzzed and she pulled it from her purse. It was a secure file from an old friend with the Mossad. More information on Jakov Koprivica. This one came from a Russian source. It confirmed their previous information. This guy was a piece of shit. How the Austrians allowed the man to emigrate here was beyond her comprehension.

"Important?" Johann asked.

She explained this new information, but not how she had acquired it.

"You seem to still have some important friends," he said.

"If you spend enough time in the shadow game, you make contacts that can help you."

"Like Jake."

She laughed. "He still has contacts at the highest levels of government."

"Which government?" Johann asked.

"Exactly." She left it at that. Then she said, "Anica knows where you live, right?"

"Of course."

She got up and said, "Let's head back there. In case they show up without calling."

Since they had walked downtown, it took them a while to walk the mile or so across the bridge to Johann's apartment.

Once they got into the ground-floor lobby of Johann's apartment building, Sirena stopped him with a hand to his chest.

"What?" he asked.

"Did you notice the car about a block down the street?" she asked.

He shook his head.

"You need to be more observant. There were two guys inside. They were almost too obvious."

Sirena drew her gun.

Johann was a bit shocked. "What are you doing? I live here."

Although Johann refused to pull his weapon, Sirena kept her gun ready as they went upstairs toward his apartment. Something wasn't right, she was sure.

They stopped at his door. The lock looked fine, though. She waved for him to unlock the door, which he did. Then Sirena rushed in, her gun sweeping the room.

Sirena stopped suddenly when she saw the woman sitting in the chair at the far side of Johann's living room.

"What the hell are you doing here?" Sirena asked.

Sabine Bauer, Kriminal Hauptkommisar of Tirol, uncrossed her legs and set her cup of coffee on the table in front of her. "We need to talk," Sabine said.

Sirena put her gun back in its holster and took a seat across from the Polizei officer.

"Can I get either of you something stronger than coffee?" Johann asked.

"We're on duty," Sabine reminded her officer.

Johann checked his watch and then said, "Since I'm currently assigned to Europol, my hours are different. We worked late last night."

"And you will be working late tonight as well," Sabine said. "Now, sit down."

Johann took a seat on the sofa.

"We have a problem," the Polizei officer said.

"Koprivica," Sirena said.

Sabine lifted her chin with acknowledgement. "He has friends in high places."

"I figured that much," Sirena said. "Otherwise, why let such a despicable piece of crap into Austria?"

"When he came in, our government was letting anyone with a pulse cross over and stay in Austria," Sabine said. "It's all about demographics. Europeans are like pandas. We are not breeding enough to sustain our population. So, we allow those into Austria who should never be here."

"We know this," Johann said. "It's changing Austria. And not for the better. We are losing our culture."

Sabine nodded in complete agreement. "You are right, Johann. Now, the new government has made positive changes. They have halted emigration of refugees. Made it much more difficult to come here. But Koprivica and his organization make a lot of money bringing people here and other countries in Europe."

This was not news to Sirena. It was one of the reasons she and Jake had taken a home in The Azores. "You said Koprivica has friends in high places. Do you have any names?"

Sabine shook her head. "Not yet. Koprivica was not on our radar until he was discovered by Jake, Anica and the two of you. Since then, I have looked into the man's background further—including with our intelligence sources."

"He should go before The Hague court," Johann said.

"That will take years," Sirena said. "In the meantime, someone else will fill the void. The structure seems to have been built like a military organization. When one person gets taken out, another is elevated to the next higher position."

Sabine agreed with a nod. "You are correct. If you have ever had a mouse in your house, you will know that there is never just one. At least not for long. You can't just catch one and be done. You must catch them all."

"Kill them all," Sirena provided.

"I am Polizei," Sabine said. "I must work within the law enforcement guidelines."

Smiling, Sirena said, "That's why you got Jake involved. You knew that he would do anything to find Anica. But once Jake gets on a case, he doesn't stop until he gets every last rat."

Sabine said nothing now.

Was this all a set-up from the beginning, Sirena wondered? What if Sabine set up Anica? If she had died that night on the Innsbruck bridge, she could have still come to Jake to find Anica's killer. Could Sabine be that callous and calculating? Sirena would like to hope not, but she had seen too much crap in the past to at least not posit the proposition.

"Who do you trust within your organization?" Sirena asked.

"Why?"

"Because you must trust those two plain-clothed Polizei officers in the car out front," Sirena said.

"You caught them?"

"It was hard not to." Sirena tried not to look at Johann.

Sabine hesitated briefly before saying, "They went to the Polizei academy with me. One is from Salzburg and the other from Graz. So, yes, I trust them completely."

"They are still patrol officers," Sirena surmised.

"Yes, but they were also trained in our Army. The important thing is that I can trust them."

"Do I know them?" Johann asked.

"I doubt it," Sabine said.

"You asked for them specifically. Wouldn't that alert someone that could be connected?"

Sabine shook her head. "No. Officially, they are on vacation." She stopped and shifted her gaze to Johann. "Where is Anica and Jake?"

Good question, Sirena thought. Since Johann said nothing, she took the question. "They're on their way. Should be here any moment. You better tell your men downstairs to back off."

"Why?" Sabine asked.

"Because if Jake sees them, he might be inclined to do something to them."

Sabine pulled out her phone and typed a quick text. Then she said, "They'll go a few blocks down by the river."

Sirena checked her watch. She was starting to worry about Jake. What was taking him so long? She found her phone and texted him.

29

Western Austria

Jake was in the passenger side of the Alfa Romeo, while Anica drove far too slow along the Autobahn about twenty kilometers west of Innsbruck. He had gotten the information he needed and was going over the data, while he kept an eye on the two men in the car behind them. Yeah, he had caught the men surveilling them when he came out of the bank in Lichtenstein. But in this case, he had simply let the men follow him. Why? Before they even left Vaduz, Jake had gone to the trunk to pretend to get something. That's when he found what he was looking for—a GPS tracking device. He didn't think for a second that the Italian had left it behind. No, this had been slipped in Jake's trunk by his old friend with Swiss FIS, Hans Disler, when they had transferred Caspari from the Alfa to the intel officer's Mercedes. So, the FIS wanted to have a stake in Jake's actions. He didn't blame Hans for trying. Jake would have done the same thing. Now, Jake had to decide if he should call Hans and tell him to call off his people, or simply let the men follow him as back up. He had decided to let them hang back there for now.

"Are you going to answer that text?" Anica asked.

Jake came out of his reverie. He found his phone and saw that it was Sirena. He texted back, saying they were about a half hour out.

Sirena came back at him, saying Sabine was with them, and she had called in a couple of old friends from Austrian Polizei she trusted.

'Is she sure?' Jake asked.

'Yes. Friends from the academy. Stationed in Salzburg and Graz.'

He needed to talk with Sirena, so he hit the green button to call her.

"Hey," Sirena said. "What's taking you?"

Jake explained how they had been up all night, and had to sleep a little along the way. He also mentioned their stop in Lichtenstein and the two men who were following them.

"You could have planted the GPS on another vehicle and lost them," she said.

He had done that in the past a number of times. "I know. But I trust Hans."

"Trust but verify," she said.

"We plan one more stop for gas just before entering Innsbruck," Jake said. "I'll talk to the men at that time."

"Be careful." She hung up.

That was strange. She never ended a call that way. Was she getting closer to him than he thought? Perhaps.

"Everything alright?" Anica asked.

"I think so," he said, and then explained the two men that Sabine had brought in to help.

"She must really trust these officers," Anica said. "Word is that she stopped trusting after her relationship with her former boss fell apart."

"Well, the man was married," Jake reminded her. "Was he screwing around on her?"

"That's the story."

Jake had never gotten along with Hermann Jung. He had wormed his way into the position when Franz Martini, a good friend and associate of Jake's, started having problems because of complications with cancer. Martini had been reasonable; Jung had been a total tool. Now, Jung was gone and Sabine Bauer ran the show.

"Pull into that gas stop ahead," Jake said.

"What are you going to do?"

He smiled and shrugged. "I'll improvise."

She pulled in and moved to the forward pump. Jake got out and tried his best not to look back at the car with the two Swiss intel officers inside, but he could see that they pulled into the restaurant area of this pit stop on the Autobahn.

Once he got inside the restaurant, he caught a glimpse of the passenger in the Swiss car get out and head toward the front entrance. He was a tall and strong-looking younger man. Good. That's the way Jake liked them. Probably cocky and overconfident.

Jake wandered through a shop selling everything and anything that nobody needed on their trip. He refrained from direct vision of this Swiss man.

Then Jake headed down the hallway toward the WC. Once inside, he pulled his Glock and placed it behind his right leg.

He didn't have to wait long. The Swiss man came into the bathroom and seemed surprised that Jake was waiting for him. He got even more surprised when Jake exposed his gun.

In German, Jake said, "You need more work on your surveillance technique."

The Swiss man seemed deflated. But he said nothing for now.

"I caught you tailing me shortly after leaving Interlaken."

"That's a lie," the Swiss man said.

"Your boss should have trusted me."

"I don't know what you're talking about."

"Show me your identification," Jake demanded.

The man reluctantly pulled out his wallet and removed a driver's license, handing it to Jake. Probably fake, Jake reasoned. He threw it back to the man. Then he took out his phone, snapped a quick picture and quickly dialed his old friend Hans. While he waited for the man to pick up, he attached the photo of the Swiss man.

"Jake," Hans said. "I didn't think I would hear from you so soon."

"Check the image."

A few seconds of silence passed. Finally, Hans said, "You'll have to forgive him. He's young and new to this business."

"You should have told me, Hans," Jake said. "I could have killed them."

When Jake said these words, the young Swiss man raised his brows with concern.

"Please don't hurt him, Jake. He's a good man. A bit green, but a fine officer."

"In my old Air Force days, when you called someone a fine officer, it meant that they were barely body temperature intelligence."

Hans laughed. "You have to understand. We have been trying to infiltrate this organization for a number of months. You finally gave me a break. We have an obligation to help. Our country is being used as a conduit for all kinds of bad things."

Jake knew the man was right. "What do you want from me?"

Suddenly, the second Swiss man entered the restroom and started to reach for a gun.

"No, no, no," Jake said, pointing his gun at that man. "I'm on the phone with your boss, Hans." That seemed to relieve the tension somewhat.

"Is that the older FIS officer?" Hans asked.

"Yeah."

"He's married with two kids. His wife's name is Monica and his kids are Jan and Ute."

Jake relayed this information to the older Swiss man, who breathed a sigh of relief now.

"I just sent each of the men a text," Hans said, "giving them instructions to work with you on anything you need."

Both of the Swiss men checked their phones and saw the instructions from their boss.

"I hope these men are ready for what might come," Jake said.

"Based on your history, Jake, I guess they will have to be ready. They are heavily armed."

"Can I trust them?" Jake asked.

"They will do what I tell them."

"They need to do what I tell them."

"I'll make that clear to them. And, they do speak fluent English."

Jake thanked his old Swiss friend, hung up, and shoved his phone into his pocket.

"Can you put the gun away now?" the older officer asked in English.

Sliding the Glock inside his jacket and snapping it in place under his left arm, Jake said, "We need to talk. If you actually have to relieve yourself, now is a good time to do so."

Both men shrugged and then went to the urinals.

Once they were done, Jake escorted them back out to the parking lot. The air seemed to have cooled some already as day gave way to early evening. Clouds swirled above and rain threatened to ruin the day.

Anica waited outside. She had parked the Alfa behind the Swiss VW, which made it impossible for them to leave.

"Everything alright?" Anica asked in English softly.

"Yeah," Jake said. "Hans has loaned these two men to us." He turned to the Swiss men and said, "Show me your firepower."

The older Swiss man, Otto, pulled out his keys and popped the trunk.

Jake glanced inside and saw two B&T APC9s, with multiple full 30-round magazines in foam cases. "Nice to see you use Swiss weapons."

"Of course. The best submachine guns on the market."

"That should work," Jake said.

"I see you use the Austrian handgun," the older officer said.

Jake lifted his chin. "Otto, I've used many weapons over the years. As you get older, you realize you don't need a safety. Guns with safeties are for those who think they might shoot off their own foot. But that's possible with any gun. The Glock is reliable and a dream to shoot."

"Not much to look at, though."

"Function over form," Jake said. "And be careful. You're now on her turf." He shifted his head toward Anica.

"Form is not a problem."

"Function is just as fine," Jake assured the Swiss officer. "Let's go."

Anica handed the GPS tracking device to the younger Swiss officer. The taller man's name was Gregor. "If you get lost, just call me for directions." She handed the man one of her cards, with her cell phone number scribbled on the back.

Jake got behind the wheel of the Alfa and cranked over the engine. Then he glanced to Anica in the passenger seat. "You gave the man your cell phone number?"

"He's kind of cute," she said. "I hope you didn't totally emasculate him in the WC."

"No more than usual," Jake said. Then he pulled out and entered the Autobahn, heading toward the center of Innsbruck. "Where are we going?"

"To Johann's apartment north of the river," she said. She glanced back to apparently keep track of the Swiss officers. Then she looked back at Jake and said, "Do you trust these men?"

"Trust is earned," he said. "I trust that Hans trusts them. That's something."

30

Axams, Austria

Jakov Koprivica wandered through his large house on the outskirts of this small village a short drive from Innsbruck, wondering if his path was righteous. He knew he had not always done the right thing for the right reason, but he hoped that the ends would always justify his means.

He stopped at the end of the hallway at the entrance to his large office to gaze into the full-length mirror. He didn't see himself as the older man with gray hair, who had let himself go a bit too much. No, he saw himself as the young Serbian Army officer who filled out his uniform with mostly muscle. Now his jawline was obscured with adipose tissue. In fact, if he was being entirely honest with himself, much of his body had transposed from honed steel into a corpulent mass. The muscle was still there, he knew, but it was simply covered by fat.

Note to self, he thought. Remove this mirror as soon as possible.

Now he wandered into his office, which contained a large conference desk with six chairs. Two of the chairs were already taken by his men. Jakov settled into the chair at the end of the table and gazed at his two top captains. These men had served under him in the Serbian Army as captains, and had eventually emigrated to Austria as well. They knew things about Jakov from the old days that nobody else knew, but Jakov had hard evidence against each of them in case either of them got too chatty with the authorities.

Jakov checked his old military wrist watch and saw that they had just a few minutes before the secure conference call.

"What have you learned about Caspari?" Jakov asked his two men.

Neither man said a word. That was all Jakov needed to know. Now he was pretty sure that the Italian had been picked up as well by the Polizei.

"Let's make the call," Jakov said.

One of the captains used the desk phone to join the call. It was a military-grade encrypted phone, but it was also quite old, so Jakov was pretty sure that it was not as secure as he would normally enjoy.

Others in the organization joined in, with the exception of Giovanni Caspari, Goran Goluža from Konstanz, Germany, and a few other lower-level folks from France and elsewhere. The disappearance of Caspari and the raid of Goran Goluža's operation in Germany were the reasons for this meeting.

To date, only lower-level operatives had been impacted by the raids. But Jakov and others were concerned. There were new players in the game, and these people seemed to have a couple of things in common—they showed a certain level of competence, and they seemed to be working outside of the normal Polizei establishment.

Each upper-level leader gave a brief update of his operations. Some countries, like Germany, were represented regionally by multiple leaders. Southern Germany was now represented by a cousin of the former leader, Goran Goluža, who was still recovering in a hospital from a gun-shot wound. From there, Goluža would surely go to jail for some time. He had, after all, been caught with a number of migrants, along with a significant stash of drugs.

Jakov finally asked the obvious question. "Who is responsible for these raids?"

Silence.

Then came the voice of someone who normally just listened to these conversations. He was known only as 'The Consultant.' Nobody knew his real name. Nor did they know his country of origin. But based on his language and accent, Jakov had guessed the man was either Dutch or German. This man said, "We have an idea."

Nobody said a word. They were all waiting for an explanation.

"According to my sources, this man is a ghost. A former intelligence officer. A legend."

"But who is he?" Jakov asked.

"We don't know for sure," the consultant said. "We do know that he has a special relationship with the Austrian government and the titular royalty."

Great, Jakov said. That meant it would be up to him and his people to stop the man. "That's not very specific."

The consultant cleared his voice and said, "That's all we know about him. But we have it on good authority that he is working with certain members of the Austrian Polizei in Tirol."

Jakov shifted in his chair and leaned toward the phone. "Are you sure?"

"Yes. And I thought you had sources in the Polizei."

"We do," Jakov assured the organization. "So, this man must be working on the edges somehow."

"Off books."

"What did the Italian know of your operations?" the consultant asked.

"Not much," Jakov said.

"But he knew your name."

"Of course."

"Giovanni Caspari has disappeared."

Jakov knew this already. "The Swiss Polizei, I assume."

"No," the consultant said. "We have contacts there. Someone else."

Who else was there? "This mystery man perhaps?"

Nobody said anything. It seemed to Jakov that the others didn't want anything to do with this man. They were stuck with their heads in the sand. Or up their own asses.

"The solution is obvious," Jakov said. "I will have to deal with this mystery man."

"This makes sense," the consultant said. "After all, he knows your name. We can assume he is heading in your direction." The man hesitated before he said, "Do you need help?"

Did Jakov need help? Not likely. "I have anticipated this action and called in more men from other parts of Austria. They are arriving now." He glanced around the table to his two captains, who both agreed with him with nods. One of them waived his cell phone, indicating he had gotten text confirmation.

"Wonderful," the consultant said. "If you need anything, please let us know."

Jakov agreed, and then the call ended rather abruptly. His man cut off their call as well.

The captains looked to him for guidance.

"Get everyone together once the others arrive," Jakov said.

"Is this the fight we want?" the senior captain asked.

Jakov gave his men a reassuring smirk. "Just like the army, you rarely get the fight you want, but you fight the one you have."

"What about the shipment coming in tonight?"

"That's just a pass-through to Munich," Jakov said. "Get word to the driver that the normal escort will be staying back a greater distance tonight."

"How great a distance?"

"All the way back here," Jakov said. "But don't tell them that."

"Yes, sir."

"That will be all. We'll meet in the great room once everyone arrives.

His two captains got up and left Jakov alone. He leaned back in his chair and finally felt a feeling of angst overcome his body. He could deal with the Polizei. They were the easy part of any equation. But the unknown was the difficult part. And this mystery man made him nervous. If he was an intelligence type, he could be a problem. Challenge accepted.

31

Innsbruck, Austria

By the time Jake and Anica got to Johann's apartment building, rain started to come down in a heavy mist. Wind picked up and drove the moisture at them relentlessly as they got out and hurried into the apartment building. The two Swiss intel officers followed them closely.

They shook off the rain and went up to Johann's apartment.

Sirena gave Jake a smile from across the room, which was essentially a kiss from a distance.

Introductions went around the room. Jake had insisted on meeting the other two Polizei officers from Salzburg and Graz, so those two were waiting in the apartment as well. Including Sabine, there were five Austrian Polizei, two Swiss intel officers, and two retired American intel officers. Nine against how many? That was the unknown. But Jake knew that it would have to be enough. If the shit hit the fan, he was sure that Sabine could call in Polizei reinforcements.

After the introductions, Johann set up his large-screen TV with his laptop and opened numerous images of the complex owned by Jakov Koprivica.

"This image was before Koprivica built a couple of smaller structures to the southwest end of the property," Johann explained.

Then Johann brought up a new image taken from somewhere above the complex. "This was taken earlier today," Johann said. "We believe these two smaller buildings are used to house his men."

"Or perhaps transient migrants," Sabine interjected. "When we go in, we must understand that there could be innocent people held there."

"Like those we found in the warehouse in Konstanz, Germany a few days ago," Anica said.

"Exactly," Sabine said. "And, by the way, excellent work with that raid, Anica."

Anica smiled demurely.

Jake broke in and said, "The weather is getting brutal out there."

"We can hold off raiding the complex until the weather breaks," Sabine said.

"Do you have authorization for the raid?" Anica asked.

Sabine let out a deep breath. "Not exactly. We will be working under emergency circumstances based on a tip."

Jake glanced at Sirena, who seemed a bit uncomfortable. Then he said, "We can't wait until tomorrow to take down Jack-off and his friends."

"We can't control the weather," Sabine surmised.

"Exactly," Jake said. "They will never suspect we'd come in during a downpour. We'll have the element of surprise. Besides, as you know, secrets are difficult to keep for long." He shifted his eyes around the room, but didn't hesitate long on any one person.

It was becoming abundantly clear to Jake that Sabine wanted him to take the lead. Leadership was a learned trait, but it came to some more naturally than others. Jake had been an Air Force officer and a CIA officer. Each position gave him the tools to lead people. Yet, experience understanding people was more important than something one could read in a book. Although Jake knew he worked better alone than in large groups, he also figured he was the best person in this room to set up a tactical raid. So, he took charge.

"Here's what we need to do," Jake said. Then he ran through the best way to get in and out with the least possible chance of failure. He broke them up into teams, positioning each at strategic locations around the compound.

"Why are we holding back on the road?" the Polizei officer from Salzburg asked.

"You and your partner will be there to call in for help if shit goes wrong," Jake said. "Besides, you're supposed to be on vacation. If anyone asks, you were coming down the mountain when you heard gunshots. You had no choice but to respond."

The Polizei officer nodded agreement.

"That's a good plan," Sabine said. "And it makes sense that Johann and Anica are with me. But you didn't mention our Swiss friends."

"Right," Jake said. "We'll need their firepower at the front breech."

"We have our vests with us also," the older Swiss officer said. "But we have no spares."

Sabine said, "We all have vests. That leaves just Jake and Sirena without protection."

Jake smiled. "I never wear them."

"Same here," Sirena said. "Too restrictive. And the Velcro always rips my nice clothes."

"We'll be fine," Jake assured Sabine. "Chances are we go in and don't have to fire a shot. What about communications?"

Anica chimed in, "All of ours work together, and they work with your system, Jake. We just need to make sure the Swiss are working with us."

"Why don't you and Johann break off with our Swiss friends."

Johann said, "We can use my bedroom."

The four of them went away, and Jake was finally able to speak with Sirena in the kitchen area while Sabine and her two academy friends sat discussing the raid in the living room.

"Is something wrong?" Jake asked Sirena.

"A lot of moving parts, Jake," she said.

"I know. I don't like it either. But we've gone in with much less experience before."

"That one Swiss officer looks like he's fresh out of high school."

"Hans assured me Gregor is good at what he does. He was an Army sharpshooter. Yeah, he's young. But we all did stuff in our youth that challenged us. Seems to me a certain woman was a chopper pilot in the Israeli Defense Forces when she was younger than Gregor."

"Good point," she said. Then she touched his arm affectionately. "We need to be careful. We're supposed to be retired."

"Semi-retired," Jake assured her. "I won't fully retire until the big sleep."

"I've seen your scars. You are not bullet proof."

"I know. And I seem to heal a lot slower now. Probably the loss of testosterone."

She squeezed down on his arm. "You seep testosterone from your pours. You should think of bottling it and selling it to all those Europeans who wear skinny jeans and hair buns."

"Sounds good. As long as I don't have to do any commercials or interact with those assholes."

"Deal." Her eyes shifted toward the others in the living room, and then back to Jake. "I really want to kiss you right now. And more."

"Down girl. We have a raid in a few hours."

"I know. And you know what that does to me."

Yeah, he did. But he also had a lot on his mind, and not just this raid. Jake knew that this man was not the end of the line. Everyone had a boss. The Italian had confirmed as much.

32

Axams, Austria

It was nearly midnight by the time Jake and Sirena parked more than a kilometer down the road from Jakov Koprivica's compound. They didn't want to drive any closer than that, or a watch would have picked up the unusual traffic at that time of night. The road that passed by the complex led up into the mountains, and nobody really had a reason to drive up there at this hour. In all, they had arrived in four cars, with Jake and Sirena in the rental Alfa Romeo, Anica riding in Johann's car, the Swiss in their car, and the three other Austrian Polizei officers in their car.

Now, they sat in their cars doing a comm check, since the rain outside was still coming down in sheets. Jake wished he had one of his assault rifles for this mission, but his two handguns would have to be enough. Luckily, Sabine had acquired a couple of HK MP7s with multiple 30-round magazines of 4.6 x 30mm hollow points. Sabine gave these to Anica and Johann, while she would use her 9mm Glock. To minimize crossfire, Sabine, Johann and Anica would come in from the back to secure any possible counter attack from the two small bunkhouses on the property. Jake, Sirena and the two Swiss officers would come in from the front.

The plan secured in all of their minds, they got out into the rain and started the one-kilometer hike toward the large chalet-style house up the road. The two other Polizei officers would eventually close off the road with their car. The road was narrow enough with the other parked cars on either side that all they would have to do was pull their car into the center of the road and turn on their portable lights.

"Nice night for a walk," Jake said over his comm.

"Maybe for a duck," Sirena said.

As they got closer to the house, Jake said, "Final comm check, One."

All the others spoke up by number, from two to nine.

"Here we go."

Jake, Sirena and the two Swiss officers split off down a side road toward the entrance of the house, while Sabine took her young officers farther up the road. They would come in from the high ground. Jake wished he had a few more people to cover them from the road up high, but he had instead kept the two officers down the road. Besides, they would have been too exposed on the hill with very little natural cover.

The four of them rounded a corner and moved along a sidewalk. Here only a couple of other houses sat on large lots, their properties covered by fences with thick shrubs, allowing them to pass unnoticed. Sabine's intel of the front had been good.

Jake could see the large house ahead. Jakov Koprivica believed in privacy and security. His fence was higher than his neighbors, and the shrubs and trees much thicker. He also had an electrically-controlled gate. But, according to Sabine, there was no security. At least not any connected to the Polizei system. Which didn't mean that Jack-off didn't have his own private system with motion detection. After all, the Italian had a system on his place in Switzerland. As did the Serb in Germany.

The only thing Jake and his crew could do was move as fast as possible. Private systems generally had a little lag, since they ran on wireless networks. Instead of crossing in front of the gate, which would more than likely have a camera, Jake and his crew stopped at a stone section of the wall. The four of them helped each other over the wall and they crouched down on the other side.

Jake whispered that they were over the wall and in place.

•

By the time Anica heard Jake say they had gotten over the wall, she was the first to make it to the edge of the compound. Their fence was only about chest high, which allowed for a nice mountain view from the back of the house. At this time, though, there were only a couple of small lights visible at the front entrance of the two smaller structures. The main house seemed completely dark.

Sabine and Johann caught up with Anica after crossing the fence.

Sabine said, "In place around back."

Then the boss motioned for Anica and Johann to spread out on either side of the lawn. But they knew not to get too close, since there would likely be motion detectors.

Anica moved swiftly across an opening and took up a position along the far fence line. So far, no lights came on. She said she was in place, and Johann followed up also. Anica was a little concerned about Johann. He had frozen in the past under pressure. How would he hold up now?

•

Without vests, Jake knew that the Swiss officers should lead the way. But he didn't always do the logical thing. He suspected his experience and reaction time would be more important to their mission.

Jake tapped the others and headed toward the front of the house, saying into the mic they were on the move.

In a straight line, Jake pushed toward the main house, keeping their signature as small as possible. All was going well until they got within a few feet of the house. A light didn't go on, but Jake could hear an alarm sound inside the house.

"Move, move, move," Jake said.

Instead of breaching the front door, Jake went to a set of French doors, not even hesitating to check if it was locked. He simply smashed his boot into the lock area, smashing glass and breaking the door frame, the doors swinging quickly inward.

Jake vectored to one side, allowing the older Swiss officer to move in while he covered them.

The outer door suddenly opened and back lighting allowed them to see a long gun.

The Swiss officer fired a three-round burst from his submachine gun, dropping the man.

Now the Swiss officer led the way into the main area of the house.

The alarm continued to sound loudly.

The Swiss officer hesitated, until Jake tapped the man on the shoulder to move forward as planned. They would methodically clear the first floor before moving on to the second level.

But the main level quickly became a shooting gallery as more men showed up with submachine guns and handguns, firing with abandon, as if they had a true target. But they made themselves targets with their muzzle flashes.

The four of them held tight cover and picked each shooter off as they moved along the edge of the living room.

Suddenly, a man appeared from the kitchen area and fired twice with his handgun, hitting the young Swiss officer and dropping him. Jake returned fire and dropped the man in his tracks.

Sirena checked on the Swiss officer, who was winded but not hurt seriously, since the bullets struck his vest.

"I'm all right," the Swiss officer said as Sirena helped him back to his feet.

"We have a problem out back," came a woman's voice over the comm, barely audible over the sound of the alarm going off. It sounded to Jake like Anica, but it could have been Sabine.

"What is it?" Jake asked.

No answer. Just gunfire from the back yard.

•

It took just a short while after the alarm sounded until the men started rushing out of the first small building out back.

Anica waited for a signal from her boss, knowing that Sabine Bauer would follow Polizei protocol from this point forward. While she waited, she said over the comm that they had a problem.

Sabine yelled that they were Polizei, but that only gave the men something to shoot at. Once they fired on Sabine's position, Anica returned fire with a full auto spread, knocking down a couple of the men who were firing on her boss.

The other men approaching started to spread out across the open grassy area, moving swiftly to covered locations.

Finally, Johann got into the game, firing a sustained salvo toward those men seeking shelter.

Now, Anica felt pinned down. But so were the other men.

•

Jake nudged up to Sirena and said, "I'm heading upstairs after Jack-off."

"I'm coming with you."

"No. You need to cover me from here."

Jake swapped a partially used magazine for a full one, shoving the old one in his pocket in case he needed it later. Then he tapped the Swiss officers on the shoulder and said he was going upstairs. With one quick motion, Jake rushed around the corner and angled around the wrought iron banister. Bullets started flying in his direction, hitting the metal and the wall behind it.

The Swiss officers and Sirena returned fire, squelching the incoming gunfire toward Jake. By now, he was up the stairs and moving with purpose. Based on the layout of the house, the master suite would be up and to the right. He hugged the wall away from the open balcony. Somehow, over the noise, he either sensed movement or heard something. He turned just in time to see a man come out of another upstairs bedroom. Before the man could fire his weapon, Jake shot the man twice. The man crashed to the wooden floor.

Jake swiveled around now and approached the master bedroom. He suspected that Jakov Koprivica would be hunkered down inside, letting his men fight for him.

Swinging the door in quickly, Jake leaned back into the hallway as bullets struck the door and the wall behind him. Instinctively, Jake shot five times into the room before crouching low against the wall, hoping bullets would not penetrate. He knew the structure was plaster over brick, so bullets would not get through that. But the man didn't return fire.

Now Jake was stuck. He needed this guy alive to move up the ladder. There was no way this guy was the top rung.

Suddenly the alarm that had been driving Jake crazy shut down. But gunfire still echoed from downstairs and outside.

"Time to give up, Jack-off," Jake yelled in German.

The Serb yelled something back in his language. Jake only understood the part about fornicating himself.

Sticking with German, Jake said, "The entire Tirol Polizei is on your property. We know about all of your crimes." A lie, of course, on more than one front.

"Then you know I will not come out of here alive," the Serb said in German with a Slavic slur.

"You will get a fair trial."

Koprivica laughed jovially. "Right. I will not survive in jail one night."

More gunfire outside.

Then, over Jake's comm, he heard Sabine order her men to call in for back-up. Jake knew he didn't have long now. Once the uniformed force showed up in numbers, there would be no way to get this man alone. But why did the Serb think he wouldn't survive in jail? Then it came to Jake. They had played around the edges on this since Jake came back to Austria. The Serb's organization had pull within the Polizei. It was because of that possibility that he had turned over the Italian to Hans with Swiss intelligence instead of their Polizei.

Jake had to move. But first he turned off his comm unit and said, "You tell me what I need to know and I'll let you go."

Koprivica laughed. "Sure. And we can go out for a beer."

"I'm not Polizei," Jake said.

"Then what are you? The mystery man, I know."

"A semi-retired private citizen." The truth.

"Hard to believe, considering you came here with the Polizei."

"Someone tried to kill my...niece. I couldn't let that stand."

"The undercover Serbian woman who went in the river? Yeah, we know about her."

"How?"

Silence.

Jake needed to see this man up close to judge his facial expressions. "I'm coming in."

"You are crazy. I will kill you."

"No, you won't. You need to know how I know what I know." Jake checked his gun. He had only fired a few rounds from this fresh magazine.

Sporadic gunfire continued downstairs and out behind the main structure. But, since Jake had turned off his comm, he had no idea what was going on.

Jake peered around the door frame and saw only the man's head on the far side of a large bed. His eyes scanned the room for anyone else, but Jake guessed the man was alone.

"You don't look like Polizei," Koprivica said. "Your hair is too long. Plus, you should be retired by your age."

Ouch. "I told you. I'm just a concerned citizen. Nobody messes with my friends or family." He brought his gun a little higher as he moved around the back of the bed.

"You have a lot of balls," the Serb said.

Jake ignored him and said, "I have friends in high places. I could get you extradited to The Hague."

Koprivica shook his head and smirked. "For war crimes? They are a joke. I did what every good soldier does. I followed orders."

The oldest excuse in history, Jake thought.

"I just need you to name your boss."

"What difference does it make? I'm dead either way."

"So, you want your boss to go free? Why not stick it to the man?" Jake wondered if that translated properly into German, and decided it worked in any language.

The Serb seemed to be considering Jake's plea. "I tell you and you let me go?"

"That's right." Jake moved around the end of the bed and noticed that the man was bleeding from a stomach wound. Jake had taken bullets to his gut in the past, and it wasn't a pleasant feeling.

Finally, Koprivica said, "I don't know his name. I know that he is probably a German man."

"That narrows it down to about forty million people," Jake mocked.

"But you mentioned The Hague," the Serb said. "He works there."

"At the world court?"

Koprivica shook his head. "The Euro Polizei."

Crap! "Do you have a name?"

"We just call him The Consultant," Koprivica said. By now the man's words were coming out much more forced, and dark red blood appeared at the side of his lips.

A liver shot, Jake thought. This man wouldn't last long.

"Is there anything more you can give me on the German?" Jake asked. "Have you seen him?"

Koprivica shook his head. "We have only talked on conference calls. Secure lines."

"How do you know he works for the European Union?"

Gunfire downstairs seemed to be slowing. But now Jake could hear Polizei sirens in the distance. He didn't have long.

The Serb could barely hold his body in a sitting position, his gun held loosely in his right hand. "You promise to put a bullet in my head?"

"Yes," Jake lied.

"He has a noticeable stutter," Koprivica said, his words more labored now. "It only comes out when he is concerned or pissed off." He hesitated and looked Jake directly in the eye. "Now shoot me."

"I can't do that."

"You promised."

"It must be self-defense," Jake said.

Koprivica grasped his gun with all his power and raised it toward Jake.

Without hesitation, Jake aimed and shot the man in the forehead, slamming the man onto his back and against the wall at the head of the bed.

Jake heard a gasp and he turned his gun toward the door. He immediately realized it was Anica, who had just watched him shoot Jakov Koprivica.

Anica moved into the room, her gun scanning for any problems. "Your comm isn't working."

He tapped on his comm and said, "It must have gotten turned off when I slammed against the wall outside. It's working now." Then he ran his hand across his throat and turned off his comm again.

She lowered her gun toward the floor and got the hint to turn off her comm as well. Then she said, "Did he tell you anything?"

Jake hated like hell to lie to Anica, but that's exactly what he did. "I told him to put down the gun or I'd have to shoot him. He raised it toward me and I fired. I had no choice."

"I saw that much," Anica said. "I meant before that."

Shaking his head, Jake said, "He was mumbling something in Serbian about screwing myself. At least that's what I think he said." He wasn't sure she was buying his story. "What's going on downstairs?"

"We rounded up a few men," she said. "Most are Serbs. But we have a few others from other countries. Before I came into the house we found a number of migrants locked in the other small building."

"Where are they from?"

"Not sure. Somewhere in the Middle East. They carried no papers or identification."

That made sense, Jake thought. "That's how Jack-off probably controlled them. He could strip them of their identity and then promise new IDs once they got to their final destination. Any idea where they were going?"

"Germany."

"How many?"

"Ten. Eight men and two women."

Jake knew they might all be alright, but if just one of them was planted as a sleeper, and that person hooked up with a few more from other groups, they would have an active terrorist cell. "What will you do with these people?"

"Our government now has a policy to return all refugees to country of origin," Anica said. "We have linguists who can determine where they are from. Then, we put them on a plane and send them back."

Catch and release, Jake thought. They were like the Mexicans of Europe.

Anica put her gun into the holster on her hip and adjusted her submachine gun on the sling over her shoulder. "Now what, Jake?"

"I believe you got the top man in the organization in Austria," he said. "But this is not over. This is like Whack a Mole."

She looked confused.

"Think of a nice grass field with a bunch of mole hills. One pokes its head up, you try to hit it with a stick and then another one pops up a few feet away."

"I don't like moles."

"Nobody likes moles."

She stepped closer to him and asked, "What do you think I should do now."

"Help interrogate any of the Serbs still alive," he said.

"I mean after everything settles down."

This was an easy one for Jake. "Stick with the Austrian Polizei."

"Why do you say that?"

"Because it seems like Europol is a political mess," he said. "I'm not sure of the efficacy of the European Union. A centralized government agency that doesn't even speak the same language is destined for failure. Look at the old Soviet Union. Despite their best efforts at Russification, they were still never able to bring in the Stans completely, not to mention the Baltic States. The Roman Empire had similar problems."

"That's good advice."

Jake turned his comm back on and said they had Jakov Koprivica. The next couple of hours were spent explaining their actions. Sabine Bauer took the lead on that front. It was her operation. Which is why she decided who knew about it and who was left out. Her boss was pissed off, but he would get over it, Jake guessed. Especially after they found out she had dismantled a large organization shipping migrants into and through Austria. But not just the people trade. Sabine, Anica, Johann, and the two other Polizei officers from Salzburg and Graz would get credit for stopping a huge drug and gun-running operation on Austrian soil. Anica, of course, would get credit for efforts in France, Germany and Switzerland also.

Anica went off with her Polizei duties. She would be busy for quite a while trying to extract more information out of the Serbians.

Jake met Sirena down on the first floor of the chalet. The place looked like a scene out of a horror movie, with dead bodies sprawled about, blood spatter across white stucco walls and tile floors.

Sirena smiled when she saw Jake. "Are you alright?"

"I should be asking you that," Jake said. "It's like a butcher shop down here."

"Butcher shops are cleaner than this," she assured him.

"Anyone on our side hit?"

"The young Swiss officer, Gregor, was hit in the leg. But he'll be alright. I understand Johann took a couple of shots to his vest. One solid and one glancing blow." Sirena hesitated as she glanced about the room. "Can we get back to our quiet life in The Azores now?"

"Yeah. I could use a little fishing right now."

"I was thinking about some good wine."

"Red?"

She glanced at the blood and said, "I think white would be better."

33

Innsbruck, Austria

Less than thirty hours after the raid of the Serb's compound, Jake entered the Tirol Polizei Station commander's office on *Kaiserjägerstraße* 8. The outside of the three-story building reminded Jake of a World War II-era military building, but at least they had updated the interior.

Sabine Bauer, dressed now in her full dark blue Polizei uniform with gold buttons and epaulets, met him in the center of the room and shook Jake's hand professionally. Then, breaking protocol, she gave him a warm embrace before returning to her chair behind a large oak desk.

Jake had been in this office before when Franz Martini had occupied the position. Not much had changed, with the exception of the types of awards hanging on the wall. Franz had been a military man before joining the Polizei, so his wall showed various awards from his time in the army.

Taking a seat across from Sabine, Jake said, "Everything alright?"

She let out a heavy sigh. "My boss in Vienna is not happy."

"At your actions or your results?"

"My actions." She clasped her hands on the desk in front of her. "But he has found it necessary to take credit for me, saying he had authorized my efforts."

"I could make a few calls to Vienna and make sure you get the credit you deserve," Jake said.

"No, that's not necessary. I don't care about my career at this point. Tirol is my home. To rise any higher, I would have to take a position in Vienna. That would just about kill me."

"I understand. But you saw a problem and you fixed it. You also could have saved the life of my young friend, Anica Senka."

"She's a special young lady," Sabine said.

"Yes, she is."

"I have already put her in for our highest medal, with gallantry."

"That's great," Jake said. "She deserves it."

Sabine cocked her head to the right slightly. "You have this ability to see the complex and translate it into something much simpler."

He had been told that in the past. "It's the human condition, Sabine. When pushed, people tend to do what's in their best interest, regardless of the consequences."

She leaned forward on her desk. "Tell me about what Jakov Koprivica told you before he died."

They had already gone over this a couple of times in the past thirty hours. "I told you. He was in a lot of pain and rambling in Serbian, which I don't understand."

"I see," she said, but obviously didn't believe.

"Have you gotten anything from those we brought in?" Jake asked.

"We put two of them together in a cell and had Anica monitor them," Sabine said. "So far, the one who had been a captain under Jakov Koprivica, had told the other one to keep his mouth shut or the organization will do it for him."

"You think they have that kind of pull within your jail?"

Sabine smiled. "We're working on that."

"There was a mole somewhere in this building," Jake assured her.

"Perhaps. But it could have been somewhere in the reporting structure, from here to Vienna. We will find the leak."

Jake had a feeling she was right. But he also guessed the leak didn't move to the east, but instead drifted toward the north.

"Is your girlfriend still in Austria?" Sabine asked.

"No."

"She's back in The Azores?"

Jake lifted his chin and nodded.

"Maybe we could have a drink before you leave," she said. "With Anica and Johann, of course."

"That would be great," Jake said, and then got up from his chair. He reached across the desk and shook

Sabine's hand one more time. It was nice to know that he had a friend in the Tirol Polizei who could keep an eye on Anica. An advocate.

He headed toward the door and stopped, turning back to Sabine. "Take care of Anica." It came across as more of a warning than a request, and that was his intent.

Sabine gave him a half smile and lifted her chin.

When he got to the ground floor of the Polizei station, Anica was waiting for him in the lobby. She was dressed in civilian clothes, having been ordered to take some time off.

"Everything alright?" Anica asked.

"Yeah. Just great."

"I got a text from Sirena," she said. "She's back in The Azores. She couldn't wait for you?"

"No. I plan to visit my son, Karl, for a few days."

"He's with the diplomatic corps, right?"

Something like that. "He's on a stopover in Germany, so we plan to drink a little beer."

"I wish we could meet," she said.

He would like nothing more for them to meet, but he knew the situation was impossible, considering the nature of Karl's work. "I'll set something up in the future. What about you?"

"What about me?"

"Will you still be working with Europol?"

She shook her head. "Not likely. This will be my Polizei uniform now. I was offered a position in EKO Cobra, but decided against that. Only one woman has made it through the training."

"Counter terrorism is a good position," Jake said. "But you have a brilliant mind for detection. You're better suited there. More likely to advance there as well."

She agreed with a smile.

"Well, I need to head out," Jake said.

"Where are you going in Germany?"

"Berlin," Jake said. He hated lying to her, but there was no way around it.

"Are you flying or driving?"

"I'm taking the Alfa Romeo. The Autobahn is calling my name." That was the truth.

"Do you want some company? I have some time off."

"I would love it," Jake said. "But my son has a very narrow window of opportunity."

She smiled. "Oh. He's not really a diplomat."

Jake shrugged, leaving it like that.

Anica moved in and gave Jake a massive hug, holding him tight to her body. When she finally pulled away, Jake kissed her forehead. She had tears coming from each eye, which she wiped away with the back of her hand.

"I'm sorry," she said.

"For what?"

"Being so emotional."

"There's nothing wrong with that, Anica."

"It's just that I really have no one here," she admitted.

"You always have me," he said, "even if I'm far away. Just call me or text me. Very few people have my number. I will always be here for you."

"I wish you lived in Innsbruck again."

"Summers are great, but I've become used to milder winters."

"You've given up skiing?"

"I haven't done much since I got my knee shot up years ago."

"I understand." She gave Jake a quick kiss on both cheeks. "You come back soon."

"I will. And you're always welcome at my place in The Azores. Come to visit us."

"I would love that."

They hugged one more time, and then Jake turned and left her in the lobby as he went to retrieve his rental Alfa Romeo.

Just as he sat behind the wheel of the car, he got a text from Hans in Switzerland. His men had gotten back and were debriefed. Hans wanted to thank Jake for allowing his men on the operation. The Italian Jake had turned over was still providing intel. He was the gift that kept on giving.

Jake cranked over the engine and listened to the roar of the machine. Yeah, he guessed the Autobahn was calling him. But not Berlin.

34

The Hague, The Netherlands
One week later

Jake had not visited his son Karl. He never intended to do so. In fact, he had no idea where his son was currently assigned with the CIA.

Instead, he had traveled north through Germany, testing the engine and handling of the rental Alfa Romeo. The car had performed as advertised. He thought about Karl's mother, Toni Contardo, and how she had almost always owned an Alfa.

Once Jake got to The Netherlands, he had found a place to stay as close to his target as possible. The man lived only two kilometers from Europol Headquarters.

Jake had no problem getting close to the German. Arrogance was a pesky habit to have for a man in his position. It allowed him to be patterned and approached without much concern.

Verner Kappel was Deputy Director of Operations at Europol, yet he had no security detail when he picked up his morning coffee and pastry at the bakery a few blocks from his house. He had no security at the gym a kilometer from his house, either. Or at the restaurants he frequented.

Kappel was a creature of habit. Not a good trait for security, but an easy target for Jake.

And Jake had done a deep background on the man. He had been married, but his ex-wife still lived in Hamburg. His two daughters lived in Berlin, and Kappel only saw them on holidays. The man lived alone in a two-story stand-alone house, the grounds fenced and covered with shrubbery and thick trees.

Security would not be a problem, Jake knew. He would not need to breach anything, since his benefactor, the Spanish Billionaire, ran the security company used by Kappel. Jake had been able to disarm the system electronically.

More importantly, perhaps, was the electronic surveillance Jake had conducted over the past week with the help of some old friends. Now he knew he had the right man. A man who was not only arrogant, but out of control.

Jake had set up an actual meeting with Verner Kappel, under the ruse of an interview with a respected German magazine. Keeping the cover semi-real, Jake came to the man's door with his duffle bag over his shoulder. But instead of camera equipment, Jake's bag was filled with dirty laundry, a spare gun, and four full extra Glock magazines of 9mm rounds.

Kappel came to the door wearing casual Sunday clothing, designer jeans and a gray cashmere sweater.

"Nice house," Jake said in German.

"Thank you," Kappel said. "I wish I could say it was mine, but it came with the job."

The German escorted Jake into a first-floor study, where books lined two full walls from floor to ceiling, with a requisite ladder on rails.

Kappel moved around and sat behind a massive cherry desk and waved for Jake to take a seat in one of two plush leather chairs on the opposite side.

Jake set his bag on the floor, unzipped his leather jacket, and took a seat.

"Can I get you a drink?" Kappel asked.

"Thank you, but I think we should get right to the interview," Jake said.

Nodding his head, Kappel said, "You don't mind if I drink."

"Not at all." Jake took out his phone and set it on the edge of the desk, hitting the record button. "I hope you don't mind. My memory is not what it used to be. And I will be sure to send you a copy of our conversation so there is no misunderstanding."

"No p…problem," Kappel said.

Finally, the slight speech impediment came out. Jake had heard this stutter and stammer over the past few days through electronic surveillance. It was nice to confirm in person.

Jake asked some simple questions, like name and spelling of his name. Then he confirmed the man's background, from his hometown to his education and finally his Polizei affiliation. With Jake's background, he was able to name drop several people within German Polizei.

Finally, Jake said, "Why do they call you the consultant?"

This made the guy do a double take, followed by a couple of starts that were interrupted by a long string of stuttering. Kappel was rattled.

"Are you alright?" Jake asked.

"I don't understand," Kappel said. "I am the deputy director of operations for Europol, the law enforcement branch of the European Union. I am not a consultant."

Nice recovery, Jake thought.

"Pardon me," Jake said. "I was under the impression that some called you the consultant. People like Jakov Koprivica and Giovanni Caspari."

The German took one fist in the other and seemed to be squeezing the blood from it. "I don't understand."

"Sure, you do, Herr Kappel," Jake said. "You have communicated with these men a number of times using that phone on your desk."

"How?" Kappel said. Then he seemed to have a revelation and kept his mouth closed.

"Would you like for me to show you the phone records?" Jake asked.

Kappel said something under his breath, but it was too quiet for Jake to hear.

"Excuse me?" Jake asked. "You will have to speak up."

"This interview is over."

Jake shook his head. "I'm just getting started." He hesitated for a response, but the German seemed somewhat deflated. His eyes shifted about like a paranoid drug addict.

Kappel picked up his phone and was started to punch in a number. "My security will be here within a minute."

Smiling, Jake said, "No, they won't. Check again. Your phone doesn't have a dial tone."

The German tapped on the phone trying desperately to get a tone, but he couldn't. In the end, he set the phone back in its charging station. Reaching into his coat pocket, Kappel pulled out his cell phone and tried to find the number for his security detail. Once he found it, he tried to connect, but the call didn't go through.

"This makes no sense," Kappel said with a stutter. "I have no signal."

"It's being jammed," Jake said.

"Who are you?"

Jake smiled. "A concerned citizen."

Finally, Verner Kappel seemed to understand. "You are the man. The shadow who has tried to dismantle the organization in France, in Germany, in Switzerland, and in Austria."

"Which organization?" Jake asked.

Kappel tightened his jaw and tried to smile. "You have nothing on me."

"That's where you're wrong," Jake said. "We have you communicating with Goran Goluža, Zoran Petrovic and Fritz Giger. All of these men are under arrest or dead for transporting illegal immigrants, drugs and weapons across national borders."

The German put his hands in his lap. "The policy of the European Union is inclusion. The same with our member states."

"Germany is the size of one American state," Jake said, "Yet, it has over eighty million citizens. How much more can it take?"

"As much as necessary."

"For what purpose?"

"People come to Europe from war-ravaged countries with despotic dictators."

"True. Some of them. Maybe even most of them. But it just takes a few slipping through the cracks to blow the shit out of our cities, or drive a truck into a crowd of innocent people. If the people can't gather peacefully and drink beer and eat good food during a celebration, what kind of life have they given up?"

"What would you do? Build a wall?"

"Without borders you have no countries, you have chaos," Jake said. "You also have no identity. And in a couple of generations you will no longer be speaking German in Germany. Your two girls better start learning Arabic."

"That's absurd," Kappel spit out.

"No, I'm afraid that's the reality. Poland already understands this. Austria is beginning to see the light. And soon, you will no longer have a European Union. The Brits are only the first to splinter away. Others will follow soon."

Kappel shook his head. "You are a xenophobe. A racist."

"No," Jake said. "I just believe in countries with borders. Without a centralized overlord of unelected officials like the EU imposing their will on the people of the member states."

"These people deserve a home," Kappel said.

"God gives us all the right to life and liberty. But that doesn't mean people have the right to take up residency in any country of their choice. These people need to stand up and fight for their homeland. Kick out the dictators. If they are not willing to fight for their home, then they can't blame God or other countries for their plight."

Jake saw the movement and knew what was coming.

Kappel tried to draw his gun from his desk drawer. But, as if in slow motion, Jake caught the black handgun rising toward him.

With one swift motion, Jake drew his own gun and shifted to his right.

The first round from the German's gun whizzed by Jake's head and struck the wall behind him.

Jake fired three shots. The first one struck Kappel in the chest, the second blew a hole in the man's neck, sending an instant stream of pulsing blood from the wound, and the third bullet struck the German just above his right eye.

Somehow, Kappel managed to fire a couple of more rounds, but both struck the ceiling.

Jake stood tall and watched as blood flowed freely from the German's chest and the neck wound went from spurting to seeping.

When Jake sensed movement at the door, he swiveled around and aimed his gun at a man entering with his gun aimed at Jake.

"Hey, Shaggy," Jake said. "I had a feeling you would eventually show up."

"You just murdered the second highest ranking officer at Europol," the younger man said.

"For the record," Jake said, "Verner Kappel pulled his weapon and tried to kill me. I simply defended myself. Now, Rolf Fischer, aka Shaggy, why are you pointing your gun at me?"

"You just executed my boss," the Austrian Polizei officer and Europol officer said.

Jake shook his head. "Do you see that phone on the desk?"

The Austrian took two steps closer, his eyes shifting toward Jake's phone. "What about it?"

"The phone is not just recording our conversation," Jake said. "It is uploading the file to the cloud. It is also connected to the Austrian Polizei. So, you might want to put down your gun."

"I could just shoot you," Rolf said.

"You might get one or two shots off," Jake admitted. "Then I'll be forced to kill you."

"You're pretty sure of yourself."

Jake shrugged. "Confidence comes through experience. Now, put your gun down."

Rolf Fischer was considering his options. Finally, obviously not wanting to die, the young Polizei officer set his gun onto the low carpet.

Then Jake directed the man to his knees with his hands behind his head. Jake found zip ties inside his pocket and he bound the officer's hands behind his back. Then he also strapped his ankles together. Finally, Jake strapped the young man's hands to his feet like a hog ready for the pit.

Now Jake found his phone on the desk. He stopped the recording and then slowly wandered out of the large house. Once he was outside and heading toward his car, Jake sent a link to the recording to Sabine Bauer in Innsbruck. In the text, Jake mentioned Verner Kappel was dead and Rolf Fischer was tied up in the first-floor study.

Sabine texted back saying she would handle it. She thanked him for his help.

Jake found the rental Alfa Romeo down the street. As he slowly drove off, he could hear the distinct sound of sirens approaching.

35

Pico Island, The Azores

Jake had dropped off his rental car at the Amsterdam airport, where he had coordinated a flight in the Spanish billionaire's jet. On the flight, he had heard from Sabine Bauer that the local police in The Hague had taken Rolf Fischer into custody and had promptly transported the man back to Innsbruck, turning him over to the Tirol Polizei. Shaggy was squealing like the stuck pig he had become, saying he was simply following the orders of Verner Kappel. But Sabine wasn't having that.

She had linked Rolf to the leaks in her organization. He was in deep shit.

Now, Jake sat on the edge of the rock formation down the hill from his small cottage, his fishing rod propped in a fissure. The sea was calm with slow, steady swells moving out with the tide. The sun was nearly at the horizon, but a warm breeze drifted up to Jake.

"I'm guessing you could use one of these," came a voice from behind him.

Jake turned and saw Sirena coming down the path with a bucket of ice. Sticking out of the ice were four bottles of beer.

"I think it could be beer thirty," Jake said.

Sirena set the bucket on the rock and took a seat next to Jake.

"Did you bring. . ."

She smiled and pulled a bottle opener from her pocket. Then she opened two bottles and handed one to Jake.

They sat quietly and sipped their beers as the sun slowly drifted below the horizon.

Finally, Sirena said, "How was your son?"

She knew, he thought. Had to know. "I didn't visit my son," he admitted.

"Why not?"

"I don't know where he is right now," Jake said.

"You hung back in Europe for a week. Is there something you want to tell me?"

"I'm guessing you've heard about the man from Europol."

She shrugged. "I hear things."

Jake said nothing for a moment as he drank his beer. Then he said, "I needed to do that on my own. I didn't want you involved."

"Why? I thought we were a team."

He reached over and took her hand in his. "I haven't had the greatest luck with women."

She squeezed down on his hand. "I'm a big girl, Jake. I've been doing this almost as long as you."

"I know. But I don't know if I can handle. . ." He trailed off without completing his thought.

"I don't want to end up in some nursing home wishing I had lived a more interesting life," she said.

"I don't think you have to worry about that," Jake said.

"Do you want to back off and retire?" she asked.

"Is that what you think?"

"I don't know."

She knew, Jake thought. "There's no telling what the future brings for us. We'll just have to see what happens next."

Sirena raised her brows and took a drink of beer. Then she moved closer to Jake and kissed him passionately on the lips.

Suddenly, line started to peel off Jake's reel. He slowly pulled the rod from the fissure, tightened the line, and set the hook. The fight was on.

Made in the USA
San Bernardino, CA
03 September 2018